FLOWERS FOR EMILY

A Novel

T.L. Vance

iUniverse, Inc.

New York Lincoln Shanghai

Flowers for Emily

iUniverse books may be ordered through booksellers or by contacting:

iUniverse
2021 Pine Lake Road, Suite 100
Lincoln, NE 68512
www.iuniverse.com
1-800-Authors (1-800-288-4677)

Because of the dynamic nature of the Internet, any Web addresses or links contained in this book may have changed since publication and may no longer be valid.

This is a work of fiction. All of the characters, names, incidents, organizations, and dialogue in this novel are either the products of the author's imagination or are used fictitiously.

ISBN: 978-0-595-44499-1 (pbk)
ISBN: 978-0-595-68794-7 (cloth)
ISBN: 978-0-595-88827-6 (ebk)

Printed in the United States of America

FLOWERS FOR EMILY

This book is dedicated to my family and everyone that has believed in and supported me throughout this adventure. Your time, opinions and suggestions are invaluable to my process. Also, heartfelt thanks to my Mom, forever a true source of inspiration and support, for always finding a way to give a little more when there's nothing left to give. To my pillars, Diana, Candy and Christina, for keeping me sane, especially you Di, if for nothing else, than for proving that from the pieces of even the most broken of hearts, love will find a way. To Nancy and Angela, for your tireless help with editing, and Gregg for your assistance with my cover, thank you all for your patience. Lastly, to Jeff, for bragging rights, thank you not only for being a great friend but also showing me the proper way to chase a dream.

CHAPTER 1

▼

Veronica Donavan stared at the folders laid out on the coffee table, running through the contents of each one more time in her head. She knew every intricate detail by heart, but everything had to be perfect this time. There could be no mistakes and absolutely no question of her credibility. She had to be ready for anything they threw at her. She knew tomorrow would be the hardest day. If she could get through tomorrow's cross examination, she would be able to breathe a little easier. Were she to show any signs of fumbling, she would most likely lose the one thing she had left. A sister and a husband had already been sacrificed to this case, and Roni had decided that she would offer up her career too, if it were necessary.

Nerves bunched up in her stomach and she stood to walk to the large picture window of her rented apartment. The lights of downtown Denver were beautiful against the dark outline of the Rockies, but the scenery was as unfamiliar to her as the deception she planned. Taking a calming breath she closed her eyes and rested her head against the cool glass, wakening her inner voice. It defended her actions for the thousandth time.

If she weren't sure it was him, it would be different. However, he had all but sent her a forwarding address when the killings resumed with the exact same modus operandi. She had sworn to do everything in her power to stop this maniac, and the information she carried in her head could cut the FBI's investigation time by more than half. That alone was worth a few well-laid lies.

Sighing heavily, she turned back to the coffee table and picked up the folder that always seemed to be lying on top, the face in front of her blurring through the tears that filled her eyes. Yeah, it was worth it. It was worth lying to her boss, her family, anybody. It was a means to an end, the end of a literal nightmare. Fighting off the tears that clogged her throat, she dropped the folder back on the table and rolled her shoulders to ease the tension.

The primal urge to pummel something was fierce. With a glance at the clock she started for the bedroom to change. It was a little late, but even if she couldn't find a sparring partner, she could still work on the bag for a little while if she hurried. The run-down gym the doorman had turned her on to would probably be the best thing about her trip. She had taken an instant liking to the old man that ran it and knew if it came down to it, she could persuade Pop to let her stay after closing because he understood her passion. Kickboxing had been in her blood since her single digits, and she couldn't remember a time when she didn't have the sport as an outlet for her frustrations. She was afraid tonight was going to be one of those nights that she wouldn't stop until she had completely exhausted herself, mentally and physically.

$$* \qquad * \qquad * \qquad *$$

Entering the old-world boxing gym, Dean Colby hitched up his duffel bag on his shoulder as he crossed to the counter, his dimpled smile broadening as a grizzled, old man emerged from the back room. One glance and Dean got a large, toothless grin. Pop's voice rose to be heard over the din of the room. "Looky what the cat dragged in? You have a good trip?"

Dean finished signing the ancient logbook and gave Pop a knowing look as he grinned. "I came back. So yeah, it was a good trip. Is A.J. still here?"

Pop nodded toward the last occupied ring, his grin broadening as he thought of the person already there. "Yeah, but you're a little late. Your boy found someone else who needed a sparring partner."

Dean turned and found the ring through the maze of equipment, his frown disappearing when AJ took a foot to the side of the head. A broad grin was returned to Pop as Dean leaned against the counter. "So who's the chick kicking A.J.'s ass? And don't even try to shrug up them old, bony ass shoulders. I know you already know everything about her."

Pop's grin grew sly, the cigar he constantly chewed on rolling around between his lips as he tried to look sheepish. "Well now, I don't know everything, but she's been in town for about a week, and she's stayin' over at old Henry Milford's building. You know my poker buddy, he's the doorman over there. Anyway, he said she was askin' around for a place to work out, and he told her to go to that spa over on Hillcrest, and she told him she wanted to go to a real gym, somewhere she could work with a bag or do some kickboxing. Naturally, he told her to come here. In town for a job, I wouldn't think for very long though, since she rented a furnished apartment. But she's a good Irish lass. Grew up in Dublin with two brothers, both boxers. From what I've seen, she could kick your ass too, so I'd mind myself if I were you."

Dean straightened a bit, eyes sparkling with mischief as he whistled low. "Whew, I'd hate to see what I'd get if you did know something, old man. But honestly now, you really think she can kick my ass?"

As the phone rang, Pop dismissed him with a knowing grin and wave of the hand. Dean made his way ringside, his eyes never leaving the action going on inside the ring. He had just set his bag on the bench when AJ went down again, and he grimaced when his friend hit the canvas next to him with a hard thud. Stepping forward to catch his eye, his voice was full of teasing. "You tryin' out for the divin' team, or what?"

AJ rolled his eyes, popping his mouthpiece out and giving his opponent a time-out sign. "Give me a sec?"

Sliding under the bottom rope, A.J. took off his headgear as he accepted the bottle of water Dean handed him. He took a healthy drink before answering. "You climb up in that ring with her. She's freaking ruthless, and that's saying something. I've fought you."

With a weary thought, and a longing for a beer, A.J. decided to let them go at each other and looked up at Roni over his shoulder with a grin. "You wanted a competitive bout? Your boy just walked in. Dean's our best kick boxer."

Leaning into the ropes she chuckled, and Dean wished she would take off her headgear so he could put a face with the softly accented voice that mocked him. "I don't know, A.J. That's what they told me about you."

Dean shook his head as he tried to pull AJ to the side to persuade him back into the ring. "Come on, man, I've been holed up for two weeks. I really need to …"

AJ stopped and cut him off, disbelief in his voice as he thought about what that bout with him would have been like. "You need to what? Take it out on me? No thanks, bro. The way I see it, you and Roni are perfect for each other."

Dean's efforts to stop his retreat fell on deaf ears. After a few seconds, he looked back to the woman in the ring, knowing that even if he couldn't see it, she was laughing at him. "What?"

The slight lilt in her voice confirmed his suspicions. "You gonna stand there and pout all night or get up here and take your beating like the rest of them?"

Dean grabbed his gear and grudgingly climbed into the ring, stretching a bit as he kept an eye on her as she fidgeted around. He was having second thoughts about sparring with her. Although her form was great, now that he was actually in the ring with her, she seemed so small.

Roni saw it in his eyes as soon as he met her on level ground and felt a pang of disappointment. She should have seen it coming, the doubts, the insecurities. Could she handle it? Would she fold with the first punch? She was beginning to think the only place she could get a decent workout was with her brothers because they didn't care if they beat the crap out of her. Between them, they figured the harder they were on her, the tougher it made her. Taking a pause, she tried not to let his closed-mindedness get to her. She would not get angry. She would just have to prove herself, again. It was too bad his condescending tone made her forget her pledge.

"You sure you're up for this, Shorty?" Dean wasn't sure what shocked him more, her speed or her strength, but it took only seconds for him to realize he'd better defend himself.

Roni could tell with each punch he threw he was testing her. Each one was just a little harder. And when she proved to him she could not only throw a punch but she could take one too, the bout turned to skills. She didn't take many hits. She was smaller and a lot quicker than anyone Dean had ever faced. She forced him to adjust his thinking, thus offering him an altogether different kind of challenge.

An hour and a half later Pop was shouting at them from ringside and Dean had to stomp down the spark of aggravation he felt at having to stop as he walked to the edge of the ring to better hear the old man.

"I said, if you two wanna beat each other up all night, that's fine with me, but I'm going home."

Dean looked at Roni over his shoulder, his tone implying that he didn't expect her to take him up on his offered out. "What do you say, Shorty? You ready to give up and concede defeat?"

Roni shook her head slightly, the confidence in her voice making his grin broaden. "I'm not even breaking a good sweat yet. Why would I concede anything to you?"

Pop didn't wait for an answer, his palm striking the mat with a thud before he held it up in a farewell salute. "You have a key. Lock up when you leave."

Dean gave him a nod, putting his mouth guard back in as he turned back toward his opponent with boyish enthusiasm. "Now, where were we?"

Just when Roni thought she'd found a decent adversary, Dean began to run his mouth, and she wanted to crush him. She had thought her brother, Shaun, was bad with his smart-ass remarks, but if she heard one more crack about how hard she hit, she was going to kick the man's head off. She had taken it easy on him with the legs, but now he was beginning to push all her wrong buttons.

Dean opened his eyes to see Roni leaned over him, and shook his head a little when her voice sounded hollow in his ears. "Are you okay?"

He was either dumbstruck or awestruck, but never, ever in his life would he have expected the angel leaning over him to be the hell bitch that had just taken his head off with some blows he'd never seen. He'd seen a lot of moves, too, in his time. With her headgear off, he could see that her hair was long, curling below the shoulder, and dark brown that he could tell. But there was definitely no mistaking the silver blue eyes that looked at him with a mixture of concern and amusement. He was so taken aback by her beauty that he actually reached up to touch her face. Remembering himself at the last second, he tapped the elastic band tangled in the ends of her hair with his glove as he grinned crookedly. "I guess I had that coming?"

Roni smiled as she pressed a towel to his eyebrow, feeling a twinge of guilt when he flinched involuntarily. "Yes, and now you match my mouthy brothers."

Dean looked at her in disbelief, his tone incredulous as he tried to pull her hand away for proof. "Shit, I'm open?"

Remorse crept into Roni's voice as she pulled back the towel with a heavy sigh. "Yeah, and you could probably use a stitch …"

"I don't think so," Dean said, shaking his head, his deep frown making the blood start fresh. "I'll just put a butterfly on it if it needs it."

Roni grinned at his disgruntled tone, and her own turned placating. "Come on, I can do it. It's the least I can do." Tossing her damp hair over her shoulder, she leaned down to shake her outstretched hand at him. "You can trust me. I'm not the type that would hit a man when he's down."

Dean shook his head at the thought of her administering first aid. Somehow he didn't envision having that body leaned all over him without touching something he wasn't supposed to, and he all but admitted it with his comment. "Darlin', I think it's you who can't trust me."

Roni rolled her eyes as she gave him a disgusted look, her amused voice ruining the glare altogether. "Oh God, you've gone stupid, haven't you?"

Pushing himself from the canvas, Dean wondered why it was that a beautiful woman could turn a man into a blithering idiot. Then Roni bent over to pick up her headgear and his thoughts went out the window as he obediently followed her to the back room like a puppy.

*   *   *   *

Roni found she was a little uncomfortable confined to the small room with him. It could have been the way he kept looking at her, or maybe it was how she felt about him looking at her. Regardless, being this close to a man without boxing gloves on was a bit unnerving for her, especially one as handsome as Dean. She had thought him nice looking earlier; but now that she had him under some decent light, she was a bit more appreciative of his features. He had great skin and killer bone structure, but she thought his smile was exceptional. Although she couldn't decide whether his eyes were blue or green, both rendered her a little giddy when accompanied by that much open admiration. With a steadying breath she took his chin in hand and tilted his head back, swabbing the small gash with alcohol as she collected herself.

Roni barely heard the sharp intake of air before Dean spoke, his soft voice filling the space. "So I guess since you put my lights out, you should buy me a drink?"

Leaning back to look at his expression, she quickly decided it was a mistake. Expecting to see the raw gleam of a predator, she was shaken by the mischievousness in his expressive eyes. His dimpled grin made it a struggle to keep her voice neutral. "I don't think so, Cowboy."

Dean didn't care where the conversation went as long as it took his focus off the perfect pair of breasts in his face. Try as he might to ignore them, truth be known, all he really wanted was permission to touch them. Giving himself a mental scolding, he tried to keep his tone light when he glanced up at her expectantly. "Married?"

Roni puckered the small gash above his brow together and applied the first strip of tape, a thread of warning in her voice. "No, now be still."

Dean still pulled away from her, his tone growing more curious. "Engaged?"

Roni shook her head and looked down at him in exasperation. "No, are you going to play twenty questions or get this taped up?"

Dean ignored her tone, his next question laced with blatant confusion. "Seriously involved with pending lifelong commitments?"

Roni laughed as she pushed him back against the chair to apply the second piece of tape, her tone mockingly harsh. "No, be still."

She was struck silent by the sudden change in his eyes as he looked up at her in astonishment. "Why?"

Roni opened her mouth to answer and for once could find nothing to say. A second later it didn't matter because Dean had pulled her into a scorching kiss and the touch of his lips had obliterated her thoughts. Normally she would have boxed his ears for taking such liberties. Instead she found her fingers tangled in short dark hair that had begun to curl the minute he'd started to sweat, as she returned his searing kiss with an abandon she wasn't aware she possessed. When the kiss ended she was relieved that Dean's breath was just as uneven as hers, glad to see she wasn't the only one surprised by the electricity between them as he mouthed the word "wow" before pulling her even closer for another.

Five minutes later Roni was in a state of half undress, straddling his lap, and briefly wondering what was wrong with her as she ran her hands up his bare, muscular torso. She didn't do things like this, but at the same time, she'd never met anyone who made her want to do things like this. Dean had tapped into something wild within her that had been dormant for too long, and she'd come away from his kiss with a need that was a little bit frightening. Dean's soft lips hit the spot beneath her earlobe and her thoughts dissipated as she moaned with pleasure. Her frustration toward the clothes left between them making her voice seem strained.

"Dean?"

It was her halting tone that stopped his caressing hands, his desire to have her beyond his comprehension as he took her face in his hands and kissed her passionately. His soft voice was nearly plaintive, a breathless plea for her to end his suffering. "I swear to God I'll step in front of the first passing bus if you tell me to stop."

Although she was impressed by his gallantry she didn't quite feel the same way. After two hours of verbal foreplay in the ring and then spontaneous combustion upon contact, all she wanted right now was physical gratification. The burning hunger had reached her eyes, and a growl came from low in his throat when she sat up to pull the sports bra she wore over her head, a thin veil of amusement in her husky voice. "I was just going to tell you there weren't any hooks."

It was a mixture of surprise and ecstasy that made her gasp when Dean's hot mouth closed over a taunt nipple and she found herself clinging to him as a wave of raw passion washed over her. The roll of his tongue made her dizzy as he switched from one breast to the other with a blissful sigh. A muffled prayer was spoken against her skin, barely audible through ears rushing with blood. "God, and they're real too."

Dean would have given anything for the proper setting to make love to this amazing woman, but he was too far gone and too afraid to move their party. Afraid that if he ruined the moment and gave Roni time to think, that she would come to her senses and do the responsible thing, and the closest to responsibility Dean could imagine tonight was the condom in his wallet.

With his last shred of sanity he was able to pull away. His touch was soft, plying her damp chestnut hair from her beautiful face. Searching her eyes for any sign of uncertainty, the intensity of her quicksilver gaze made his pulse race as he choked on the words in his throat.

Roni answered the question in his eyes with the barest of smiles before she leaned in to capture his full lips, the tenderness of her kiss becoming more demanding moments before she shifted herself on his lap to better accept his rock hard erection. Dean thought his brain would explode the second she did, her groan of pleasure drowned out by a low, strangled sound. His head fell against the wall with a thud and he tried desperately not to lose himself in her intense heat. She moved against him, sheathing him in her tight wetness, and he suddenly didn't know which was worse, the sensation of being inside her, or hearing her moan his name. The twining of the two was a sweet, relentless torture.

The same intensity shared in the ring had them writhing, the sound of their breaths filling the room until the first constrictions of her climax had him fighting his own. Unable to resist the way her body milked his, each thrust became harsher until he lost himself in her, and was left shuddering against her like a schoolboy. His breathing, slow in recovering, made his words more meaningful as he kissed the sensitive skin of her throat. "Damn, Shorty, that's the second time tonight you've knocked my lights out."

CHAPTER 2

▼

Dean slid his keycard through the security lock scanner as he balanced two cups of coffee, briefly wondering if Juni had missed his morning deliveries while he'd been away. He always brought her a cup of coffee on his way for practice at the firing range, staying long enough to catch up on the daily Bureau gossip. So far, it had been a decent morning for waking up alone, especially seeing as his first surprise of the day had been the disappointment of doing so. But then, he was still reeling from the fact that he'd nearly kidnapped a woman over the idea of encountering her rejection. The only invitation he had to pique Roni's interest was the one for a rematch in the ring. Nevertheless, he would take a thousand kicks to the head to get to know her better. It wasn't often he found a woman that really interested him, especially *after* sex. Not that he was a creep, he just didn't have room in his life for a woman. Usually by the third date, after numerous answered pages and work-related abandonments, women no longer desired a relationship with him anyway. They just wanted him to hang around long enough to give them satisfaction.

Lost in his wayward thoughts, he was coming up short in making way for a gurney that approached him on his way to the morgue. He wondered how it was that Juni could work down here. He'd always felt a little sorry for her for being stuck down in the basement in her lab, along with the firing range. But as head of the Forensic Pathology Lab, she said she felt more comfortable here, close to her work. Dean preferred to remain upstairs with the living, but he always made time to stop by for a morning chat with his favorite pathologist.

Pushing on the door to the lab, Dean froze when he encountered the sight of *two* women bent over the desk with their backs to him. Engrossed in a report, they had no idea he had come in. That was fine with him for the moment because Juni had company, and company had great legs. Feeling he was being intrusive, he was about to back out quietly when his ear picked up her voice. He knew that voice, and he'd been thinking about it all morning.

His brain went into a tailspin as questions came at him from all sides, the most important being what was she doing in his forensics lab? Looking at her more closely, he noted the changes in her appearance. Her dark hair was twisted up in a clip, and the small, round-framed glasses lent her an executive look, as did the expensive tailored skirt and blouse she wore. This was a completely different woman from the one he'd met last night, and that was a bitter thought that warped his mind as he stood there wondering if she would be surprised to see him.

He wanted to turn around and retreat but he hesitated too long and Juni straightened and spotted him, her smile warm as she motioned him in. "Hey, come on in. I'm glad you stopped by. I want you to meet someone." Schooling his emotions, he prayed his heartbeat would slow down a little as he handed Juni her coffee and waited for Roni's reaction.

Setting her pencil down, Roni turned, a solid jolt of sexual energy causing her smile to freeze for half a second before she slapped on a poker face. It would figure that the one time in her life she reacted to a totally irresponsible impulse, he would walk in through the door at work. Seemed her luck wasn't improving. She resisted the urge to laugh at the irony of it. Roni was shocked to see him, but she couldn't say she was surprised. She had recognized certain traits of a fellow agent the previous night, but her lust had overridden all the warning bells and she still couldn't make herself feel guilty for indulging an insane urge.

Juni took her coffee from Dean with a quiet "Thank you," her intuitive eye catching the moment between the two. They had definitely met before and she was sure it was under way different circumstances. "Dean, this is Dr. Veronica Donavan. She's on loan to us from the Violent Crimes Division of Scotland Yard. She'll be working with us on the new case. Roni, this is Dean Colby, one of our team's best agents."

Roni's smoky blue eyes sparkled with mischief as her smile grew and she shook his outstretched hand. She could vouch for that at least. "Good morning. How's the eye?"

Dean absently touched the butterfly bandage above his left eye, not surprised he'd totally forgotten about the injury. "It's fine." And to Juni's questioning gaze, he added, "We met at Pop's last night."

Juni smiled into her cup, her voice full of humor as she glanced from one to the other. "And the head wound?"

Juni didn't miss the flicker in his eye when he answered. The Deaner's ego had taken a smack down and it took everything she had not to chuckle at his sudden irritation. "Let's just say it was just an error in judgment and a reminder to never underestimate my opponent."

Roni wasn't quite sure what he had meant by that, nor did she like the slight change in his tone, but his eyes were unreadable when he looked at her and continued. "What exactly is your field of expertise, Dr. Donavan?"

Roni's chin tilted up ever so slightly as her back straightened in defense. She wouldn't be intimidated by him or any one else when it came to her work. "I'm a certified Forensic Pathologist, and I'm currently pursuing my doctorate in criminal psychology; so my field is pretty broad, Agent Colby."

Dean didn't know what her spin was but he knew he had to get away from her if he was to think about it clearly because all he could focus on was the smell of her perfume, and the memories it invoked were impairing his ability to process things. Fighting the image of his face buried in the hollow of her neck and his hands wrapped in the soft darkness of her hair, he headed to the door, his voice slightly strained as he bid his farewell. "Well then, I'm sure we will benefit from your experience. If you ladies will excuse me, I'm late for practice. See you guys at the 10 o'clock."

Roni looked at Juni with a questioning look as he left and Juni explained the meaning of his parting remark. "We have a meeting in the control room for an update on our cases at ten o'clock every day. By any chance were you the one to open Dean's eye? And why wasn't he wearing head …"

"Yes," Roni answered, still bothered by the implications she had read in his tone, and embarrassed that she wasn't the only one to pick up on the slight attitude, "and he was. I just have little feet."

Juni was unable to hold her soft chuckle, her interest piqued as she pretended to be engrossed in an x-ray. "Yeah, well, Dean has an ego, but he's usually quick to get over it too."

Roni smoothed a hand over her black, tailored skirt and shrugged out of her lab coat, not sure why she was going after the hardhead but knowing she couldn't leave things like this. "Still, I don't want to start this case with any animosity between us. I think I should …"

Juni cut her off with barely controlled amusement, motioning down the hall. "Go right, down two doors, take a left, and follow the noise."

Roni nodded, hoping that either Juni was too preoccupied to notice her nervous tension or just too tactful to mention it as she left the lab.

*   *   *   *

Finding the firing range, Roni ignored the posted signs denying her access and snatched a pair of earmuffs from the counter before entering. Quickly scanning the semi-private stalls for Dean, she found him in the last one and stood by admiring his broad shoulders while he finished his clip, noting wryly that when he did, his target was missing most of its head. Obviously he wasn't thrilled about her being here, and she took a calming pause before stepping forward to stand beside him, her quick glance picking up the angry glitter in his eyes before he threw up the wall. "I'd like to talk to you."

Dean loaded another clip with a hard hand, his voice crisp as he barely glanced at her. "I don't know that I have anything to say, Dr …"

Roni resisted the urge to pinch him and instead grabbed his arm as he raised his weapon, cutting him off. "Stop calling me that! You know, I don't think I like what you're implying about last night."

Dean abruptly holstered his gun and led her to a deserted office, shutting the door behind them before speaking. "You don't think you would have the same thoughts? Let's look at the facts here. I come back from a two-week absence and suddenly you are at my gym, in my bed, and on my case, all in a twelve-hour time period. Sorry, baby, but that's all just a bit too convenient for me."

Roni resisted the urge to chunk the earmuffs in her hand at him, her calming breath making her response soft and deadly as she glared at him. "To begin with, I've never seen your bed. Secondly, if you'd care to reexamine the 'facts' as you call them, I've been in town for less than a week and I chose to stay close to the field office. Naturally when I asked around for a place to work out, Pop's was highly recommended. I had no clue you worked for the Bureau, nor would it have mattered. My work speaks for itself, and it has on this case for two years now. So technically, I guess it would be *my* case. And lastly, I don't need to step on any man on my way up the bureaucratic ladder, so as far as last night goes, I guess you were right about that: maybe that was just an 'error in judgment.'"

Her stormy blue eyes were nearly silver, telling Dean just how passionate she felt about the situation as she turned and reached for the door. He had hoped to see her eyes turn that color again but surely not from anger, and the last thing he wanted was to be a mistake, not to her. He didn't want what they had shared to be a regret because even he had to admit, it had been something exceptional. He wasn't sure what it was yet, but it had definitely been exceptional.

With a heavy sigh, Dean moved to stop her, his eyes sincere with apology as his hand covered hers on the doorknob. "Roni, wait. I'm sorry. I'm an ass. I freaked out and jumped to conclusions, but I don't regret last night and I don't want you to either."

Roni stared at him for a minute, trying to judge his sincerity, her indecision still an issue when she surprised herself by saying, "Look, Cowboy, the way I see it, we have two choices: we both forget last night ever happened and continue on a professional level, or we can spend the limited amount of free time I'll have while here to have some fun with the chemistry between us. Whichever you choose is fine with me."

When he looked at her in shocked silence she knew she had to make an escape before her face burst into flames, and with a firm tug on the door she smiled at the dazed look in his eyes. "Think about it and let me know."

Dean blinked at the closed door while shaking his head in dumbfounded slowness. What was it about this woman that made him unable to think whenever she was in the room? Gathering his wits he returned to his practice and was miffed when his rounds fired a little quicker and his aim was just a hair off. Although they were imperfections only he would notice, the fact was that he did notice, and he did not like it.

*   *   *   *

Tapping lightly on Mason Martin's door, Dean entered when his boss motioned for him, his usual jovialness with the man taking a back seat to his aggravation. "You're bringing outsiders in without me checking them out now?"

Mason looked at him oddly as he rose from his chair and started collecting the files he needed for the team conference. "Seeing as you were incapacitated, Agent Colby, I thought myself capable of checking out Dr. Donavan's credentials. I may be old but I still remember how to run a basic background check."

Dean took a breath and collected his attitude, his tone lighter when he responded. "I'm sorry, I'm just used to knowing about everything beforehand and I was caught off guard."

Mason's hand stilled as he glanced at Dean with a knowing grin. "Yeah, so was I."

Walking around his desk to leave, Mason expected nothing else but for Dean to fall in step beside him as he continued. "She has an impressive background

with Scotland Yard, upper level security clearance, and impeccable recommenda-
tions from several government agencies. Her supervisor has only worked with her
for six months, but he felt strongly enough about her hunches to arrange for her
cooperation with our case. That says a lot there, but more importantly, I think
her theories are right on the mark and she may be the key we need to put this psycho away."

It was clear that he wasn't the only one Roni had made an impression on, and
Dean could only nod, his voice full of resignation as he sighed. "So, you really
think the cases are connected?"

That was one thing Mason was definite on. The three case files Donavan had
sent him read identical to the ones accumulating on his desk, and a serial killer in
his city was the last thing he needed. "Yes, I do." With a hand on the conference
room door Mason again looked at Dean oddly and asked him in a slightly distracted tone, "What happened to your eye?"

✻   ✻   ✻   ✻

Sitting beside Juni at the long conference table, Roni passed a disk to Tyler
Burke, grinning as he chided her for her reluctance, his boyish charm evident in
his smirk as he looked at her over the rim of his glasses.

"Come on, you can trust me. I'm 100% geek."

Within seconds after she had relinquished her disk, he had confirmed his dec-
laration. Her information was stored, sorted, and redistributed into his programs,
and Roni quickly learned there wasn't much Tyler couldn't do with a computer.
Also on the team along with Tyler was Dr. Lyn Marks, the lead profiler on the
case. Roni had known after a two-minute conversation with the woman that she
would enjoy working with her. Lyn had a very quick mind and a straightforward
manner that appealed to her.

Roni was thankful to have been in conversation with Lyn when Mason walked
in with Dean at his side, but she still could not ignore the jolt it gave her when he
took the chair next to hers. She forced herself to pay attention, making a mental
note to give Mason the respect he deserved. She was there only by his good
graces, and she intended to keep a clear mind. After all, she was already on dan-
gerous ground.

As the table settled the screen on the wall spun into action. The team logo
danced across the monitor moments before the twelve faces she knew so well
started appearing in the order of their deaths. Every one she knew by name and
by face, and the eleventh victim she knew by heart.

Roni's eyes gravitated back to Emily's face for a fraction of a second before the notebook she had sent Mason hit the table with a thud and his authoritative voice sliced into her thoughts. "Ladies and Gentlemen, I'd like to start off by welcoming Agent Colby back from his two-week vacation with the DEA." Looking at Dean he raised his voice to be heard over the chuckles around the table, his grin slightly crooked. "We hope you enjoyed it because it's the only one you're getting this year."

Sobering completely he looked pointedly at Roni, his tone once again all business as he addressed the group. "Now that we're all together, I'd like for you to meet Dr. Veronica Donavan. Dr. Donavan works violent crimes for Scotland Yard as forensic pathologist and is studying to become a criminal psychologist. She comes highly recommended by both her superiors and her professors. She has also the experience of working a case in London with striking similarities to our media-named 'Romeo' killer. The information shared prompted me to take steps to bring her here in hopes that we are looking for the same person." Pausing for a breath, he gave Roni the slightest wink to bolster her confidence before continuing. "We are, however, so convinced that she has already rented an apartment here and will stay on our team until we catch him. And with that said, I will turn the table to you and your questions."

Tyler was the first to fire and Roni smiled at the nature of his curiosity. "Why do you think the cases are connected, how did you find out about the American victims, and what are the details on which you base your beliefs?"

Roni gave him a small smile, her pride evident in her accomplishment. "Two months after the murders in London ceased, I finished a computer program that searched for the same modus operandi. It alarmed on your third victim. Murders six weeks apart, same pattern: snatch, kill, and dump. The body is always clean, scraped nails, no prints, no mistakes."

"What about the flowers? What's your theory?"

Roni barely glanced at Dean as she answered his question. "There are several charts of 'birth flowers.' There's the more common variety that everyday people associate with, then there are the more rare ones that our killer leaves with his victims. These particular types of birth flowers supposedly bloom on your birthday every year and leave you with a personal connection and so on." Taking a breath she grinned at Juni, who snorted beside her, her own sense of humor evident when she continued. "I've personally never felt a connection with a Hydrangea bush, but it's the rarity of some of these flowers that leads us to believe he grows them himself. February's flower is Forsythia, July's, the Crape Myrtle. You don't have much luck finding either in a common flower mart. But more importantly, this also tells us that he knows enough about his victims to know their birthdates. This is definitely not a random selection of girls, therefore there has to be another commonality between these girls besides blonde hair and blue eyes. We just have to find it."

Lyn sat forward with her gaze trained on the faces before them. Her mind was already swimming with scenarios, her first question being, why would he flee his comfort zone? "Your last vic, Virginia Waltham, was killed in January. Our first victim, Angela Morris, was killed in late September. That would give him less than eight months to move across the world, settle in, grow some flowers, and find his first mark. He doesn't waste any time, does he?"

The picture of Angela Morris, along with those of Cindy Norton and Leslie Harmon, popped up on the screen, making the total fifteen girls ranging in age from fifteen to eighteen that had been killed. Roni was glad that Lyn was already in accord with her thoughts. "No, he doesn't. However, even if he moved for a fresh start or for some other purpose, the last three victims are common flowers, the Rose, Iris, and Daylily. You wouldn't need a greenhouse for those. Is it coincidence?"

Juni looked over her coworkers, knowing her analysis would weigh heavily in any decision. "The method is the same, same type of strangulation, by cord or rope, and the post mortem stab wounds are all in the same direction. I've almost come to the conclusion that we're looking at the same murder weapon, but we are still comparing analyses. Dr. Donavan and I have more work to do before I can say anything for certain."

Mason took a deep breath, sat back, and looked over his task force. He hoped he was making the right decision by bringing in an outsider, but the team seemed to be pretty comfortable with her abilities so far. All eyes on him, he gave Roni a reassuring smile, his tone confident. "I expect to be dazzled, Doctor."

*   *   *   *

Roni turned off the light in the kitchen and headed back to the sofa as she studied the file in her hand. She hadn't seen or spoken to Dean since he'd left the conference room, so she assumed he had made his decision. And in turn, she had decided to bury herself in this new evidence and hope it was a path to justice. Passing the front door on her way to the living room she jumped at the light rapping noise and glanced at the silent intercom on her wall. Looking through the peephole with apprehension, she shook her head with bewilderment as she opened the door with a grin.

"Now how did you get in here?"

Dean rolled his eyes at her, his smile cocky. "Oh, please. You don't think very much of me, do you?"

Roni grinned at his implication and gestured for him to come inside, intrigued by his sudden appearance in her hallway. "No, but we already knew that, didn't we? So you've managed to find out where I'm staying, and bypass my doorman. Am I supposed to be impressed?"

When Dean turned to face her she found herself once again looking into the eyes of the man she'd met last night, and her heart skipped at the heat she saw there. Shrugging slightly, his voice softened as he grinned. "You must have been impressed sometime or another. After all, you invited me, remember?"

Roni ignored the heat burning her cheeks, looking at him in mock confusion as she fought for something intelligent to say and found nothing but a sarcastic retort. "I should have known that would come back and bite me in the ass."

His grin spread as he tugged at his tie, his eyes sweeping hungrily over her. He'd never seen a woman look sexier in a tank top and pajama bottoms. "Well, I thought about what you said this morning and I realized something."

Stepping closer, he reached out and pushed her ponytail over her shoulder, the lingering of his fingertips along her neck making her response a rushed whisper. "And what would that be?"

With her racing pulse under his fingertips Dean had no question of her desire, and it was with clear intent that he pulled her into his arms, his words a breath away from her parted lips. "I don't want to waste any more time thinking about this."

Dean's hungry kiss left her responding in kind as she wrapped her arms around his neck and molded her body to his, her low moan of pleasure fueling his hunger just that much more. Roni was glad he'd come to his senses because she hadn't been so attracted to someone in a long time and she wanted to take advantage of it before she went back home. The passion in his kiss was consuming and she wasted no time in helping him shrug him from his suit coat, and tugging at his shirt, the file folder she'd been planning to read was left forgotten beneath the trail of clothes that led to her bedroom.

Depositing Roni on the bed, Dean left a trail of kisses down her stomach as he rid her of her pajama bottoms, his hands slow to travel back up her shapely legs as he stretched back over her, reveling in her touch as she dug her hands into his hair and urged him upward for a passionate kiss. Finally dragging his lips from hers, Dean's ragged breath caught at the beauty in his arms. With her full lips swollen from his kiss and her skin flush with desire, it only intensified her features, and Dean was hard pressed to deny the passion in her quicksilver gaze. Tonight he was taking his time and his resolve was evident in his husky whisper. "I'm going to make love to you properly tonight, Roni, I promise."

His breath was warm on her ear and Roni's eyes nearly rolled back in her head when he gently tugged at her earlobe with his teeth before trailing kisses down her throat, her breathless response making him pause. "And you didn't do this properly last night?"

Raising his head Dean's grin was suddenly full of mischief, his answer making her pulse race even more. "No, proper would be horizontal, completely nude, and you quivering in ecstasy while begging me to stop."

A delicate brow rose as color stained Roni's cheeks, her voice softly seductive as she pulled him down for another kiss. "Well, by all means, carry on then."

*   *   *   *

It was much later that Roni found herself on the verge of sleep, the gentle touch of Dean's fingertips across her back combined with the rain pelting the windows lulling her into a deep relaxed state. Pulling the heavy mantle of her hair from her neck Dean looked down into her beautiful, serene face and knew when the time came, he would not want to let this one go. He could feel it in his gut.

Peeking open an eye, Roni grinned, her voice a bare whisper. "Stop it."

He chuckled as he squeezed her tighter and kissed the top of her head. "I can't help myself, you just have the most striking features I've ever seen."

Dean was sure she was still half-asleep when she responded, but he didn't care. The sound of her husky voice was like Valium to him. "My Gran used to say Emmy and I were cursed with fairy blood, but I think we were just born with extra thick eyelashes. Pale blue eyes were supposed to be the most notable feature of the fairy queen …"

His chest vibrated with laughter as he gave her a squeeze. "Oh Lord, I think you're suffering from sleep deprivation."

Her sleepy voice went defensive as she struggled to pull away from him. "Ah now, that's one thing the Irish take very seriously is their folklore; and if you're going to poke fun …"

It was Roni's lopsided grin that stopped him cold, the nagging in his brain suddenly quiet as he saw the resemblance he'd been blind to before. She and Emily had been born with extra thick eyelashes, and the same shit-eating grin. "Roni, Emily Rourke …"

The sheer pain that clouded her eyes answered his unfinished question and he gathered her back into his arms before she could shy away, her anguish evident in her sad whisper. "Was my little sister, and if it's all right, I'd like to leave it at that for now, okay?"

He squeezed her a little tighter and sighed, pressing a kiss to her temple before speaking softly in her ear. "Christ, Roni, I'm sorry."

Roni shrugged off his sympathy, her voice emotionless as she regained her composure. "Don't make this about me, Dean. I don't want that information to sway anyone's ideas about why I'm here."

Dean's brain was in a tailspin. With the differences in their names, it was surprising to learn Roni was related to the case, but her conviction was suddenly very clear, and he was careful with his wording. "I understand your feelings, Roni, and I will respect them as long as they don't interfere with the case. I hope you can understand that." When she nodded, he continued, the curiosity too much for him to bear. "So you guys have different fathers or just different names?"

Pushing away, Roni looked at him with a sidelong gaze, her quiet admission easily explaining their name differences. "Just names. I've been divorced for nearly a year now."

Propping up on one elbow, Dean watched as she lit a cigarette from the nightstand, his voice reflective. "And the kicks just keep on coming, huh, Shorty? What kind of idiot would divorce you?"

Rising, she looked at him sadly over her shoulder as she tied the belt on her robe, her demeanor beginning to trouble him as she left the room. "A smart one."

He pondered her meaning until she returned, silent as she offered him the second glass of whiskey and sat on the bed beside him. "After Emmy was murdered, I had no room in my heart for love, and what was left I poured into the case. The more I worked, the more he worked, and the more he worked, the further undercover he went. One day there wasn't a reason for us to stay married anymore. So we're not."

Dean gave her a lopsided grin. His halfhearted attempt at humor was a clever disguise to test the finality of her situation. "And one day, when this case is over ..."

Roni's laugh was short, sarcasm lacing her retort as she interrupted. "Oh no, we're very over. It was only a matter of weeks after we divorced that Wade Donavan, for all intents and purposes, ceased to exist, if you know what I mean?"

Dean's brow rose at her implications and he nodded, sorry he hadn't left well enough alone. Not because he was bothered by the information, but because he had upset her, and he didn't like the sadness that had dulled her beautiful eyes.

"Hmmm, yeah, that's pretty deep cover. But I can't say I'm overly upset to hear about it. After all, I'd be awfully disappointed in myself if I continued an affair with another man's wife."

Roni couldn't help but grin at his decisiveness, her breath close enough to touch his skin as he leaned over her to set his glass on the nightstand, his eyes full of mischief as he added hers to the table. "Really? And you'd do that?"

Dean parted the lapels of her robe, his breath hot against her skin as he softly kissed the shapely swell of her breast and looked up at her with devilish intent. "For you? Anything."

Roni's cheeks flushed at the promise behind his tone, her own slightly mocking when she asked, "Anything? Are you sure you're up for that, Cowboy?"

Fully accepting the challenge behind her words, he laughed as he rolled over with her, a strong believer of the "actions speak louder than words" theory.

CHAPTER 3

▼

Dean entered the control room and, noticing Lyn was alone, glanced at his watch to judge how long he had before the others joined them. With a quick check of the hall, he walked up behind her to lean over her shoulder, his tone casual. "Mornin', Lyn, how's the profile going?"

She gave him a questioning look as he slid the case files around in front of her. "It's pretty slow. It would help if I could talk with all of the families. What are you doing?"

Dean pulled Emily's folder and laid it on top of the pile, looking over his shoulder when he heard Juni's and Roni's voices approaching. "You need to look at that VERY closely."

Lyn opened her mouth to comment, and snapped it closed again when he looked pointedly at Roni when she and Juni walked into the room. Curious of his behavior her eyes automatically darted from Roni's laughing face to the picture on the folder. Recognition hit her like a brick and she looked up at Dean in open question, catching the briefest of nods before the others entered the room.

Lyn didn't care how Dean got the information, but for the first time she felt more positive about connecting the victims. When they found out why he had picked these particular girls, they would find out why he was killing them. She had been going through the files one at a time and hadn't gotten to Emily's yet, so she used Tyler's distracting entrance to scan the case history, noting quickly that the information was sketchy at best.

Flipping through the rest of the pages, she grew increasingly suspicious when she saw that all of the information was inadequate for a case of this detail. And what interested her more was that, according to the medical reports, Emily had been strangled by hand, and there had been no stab wounds, both of which were conflicting technique patterns for their killer.

Questions began to pile up faster than Lyn could process them and she was glad when Mason entered to distract her thoughts, although she still found herself watching Roni throughout the meeting. By the end, Lyn had counted at least a dozen times she had absently glanced at Emily's picture. Yes, there were definitely inconsistencies here and she wanted to get Roni alone before Mason noticed them. Lyn hadn't met anyone yet that would admit to needing a psychologist, and she seriously doubted that Roni had talked to anyone when her sister was killed. She was sure this lady needed someone to talk to, and she couldn't wait for the opportunity.

Rounding up her things after the meeting, Lyn's thoughts were still preoccupied when a runner brought Mason a message and he turned toward her with a small smile. "Leslie Harmon's mother has returned and has agreed to see us. Dean, take Lyn and Roni. I want them both to be there.

Roni was gathering her folders before Mason finished his sentence, and Lyn smiled at her anxiousness. At least she understood her drive now. She had once thought she was power hungry, but now she knew it was a desperate quest for justice.

*   *   *   *

Returning a couple hours later, Lyn was still lost in her thoughts when Roni's quiet question caught her attention. "Are you all right? You've been quiet all afternoon."

Lyn took a breath and gave Roni a smile, her voice apologetic. "I'm sorry. I just have a lot running amok right now up in that scary place I call my brain. I've got a ton of questions and no answers; and actually, if you have an hour or so, I'd really like to have a sit-down and talk about some things."

Roni ignored the clinching of nerves in her stomach and returned Lyn's smile, her response lightly given. "Sure, anything I can do to help."

Once behind the doors of her office Lyn refrained from launching into her questions, taking time to discuss their interview with Mrs. Harmon as Roni relaxed. Lyn wanted an easy rapport between them so she spent the next hour getting Roni to trust her, prodding her to express her thoughts and feelings about the case. In the process Lyn gained a lot of respect for Roni as a colleague, and it was with regret that she launched into her real objective. She had spent the last ten minutes trying to figure out how to segue into Emily's file and she could find none. Looking up at Roni sitting on her couch with her legs folded beneath her, Lyn's sigh was heavy with resignation. "Roni?"

The pen twirling through her fingers froze as Roni looked up at her expectantly. "What is it?"

Taking a deep breath, Lyn sat forward, her gaze direct, her voice gentle. "I need you to talk to me about Emily. I've got all of these cases here and no family to talk to. You know I need your help."

Roni instantly glazed over, her tone suspicious when she asked, "How did you find out?"

Lyn held up the file, her tone matter of fact. "From what there was of the family history, you have the same eyes, and not that we see it very much, but the same smile. Then there's the fact that while the boys will examine your security level with a microscope, they couldn't care less about your degree. But me, well, you know I'm suspicious by nature, so I checked. And for some reason, I'm not thinking Veronica Rourke-Donavan is a coincidence."

Roni blinked away a tear, her laugh full of bitterness. "No, not a coincidence, but I have been trying to keep that information low profile so there won't be any suggestions that I be removed from the case. I know how strict they are about being personally involved, Lyn, and …"

Lyn shook her head as she interrupted, knowing already that Mason wouldn't let anyone take her off this case. "With your knowledge, research, and experience, you are too valuable. There's no way they would risk more victims by deporting their best asset. Besides, I only want you to talk to me right now." Taking a breath Lyn looked back at the folder in her hand, her head shaking slowly. "There are inconsistencies here that are going to surface when her review comes up, and you know I can't push her to the back of the line forever. There will be some hard questions to answer …"

Roni knew it was coming, but she still hadn't figured out how to explain it; so what Lyn got was her gut reaction, the definitive tone of her voice backing her conviction. "He killed her, Lyn."

Roni was so used to getting shut down by her peers that Lyn surprised her by actually offering a theory. "I agree. Maybe opportunity presented itself and he was caught unprepared? I don't know, but there are significant meanings to these discrepancies—no stab wounds, he hid the body, her face was covered, all clear signs of remorse …"

Roni stood suddenly, emotion making her interruption abrupt. "I know what it means."

Lyn sighed heavily, speaking softly as Roni began to pace the room. "Was this case responsible for your interest in criminal psychology, Roni?"

Pausing for a second, Roni answered candidly, a tinge of disenchantment in her voice. "This case is responsible for a lot of things; but yes, I want to know what makes a person do this type of thing."

Lyn's sigh was heavy, her tone implying she was stating the obvious. "You'll never understand, Roni. No matter how hard you study, you'll never find the answer in a book, or a degree."

Running a hand over her eyes, Roni's reply was full of frustration. "I know."

Tapping her pencil on her chin, Lyn looked at Roni with a raised brow. "I think you also know Emily may very well be the key to unlocking this case. I don't think she was a random victim, and you think she was killed as a warning to you …"

Roni looked at her skeptically, her voice echoing the emotion. "And you don't?"

Lyn shrugged slightly, her response matter-of-fact. "No, because if he was trying to send you a message, he would have followed his rituals to prove that Emily could be just another number."

Roni hadn't taken into consideration that including Emily's case meant that she would have to talk about it, and after years of trying to get someone to listen, now she wondered if she had the courage to speak about the events that had changed her life so drastically.

Watching the war of emotions cross Roni's face, Lyn's voice turned low and pleading. "I'm sorry to put you through this, but I need you to tell me about her, Roni, everything you remember."

Roni stopped to scan the certificates and awards that covered most of Lyn's main wall, her eyes pausing on a picture of Lyn and her family at graduation. She'd once had a happy family, and she missed it so bad it hurt. Taking a steadying breath, she reached up to wipe away a tear before responding. "It would take too long to tell you everything I remember about Em. She was a great kid: smart, beautiful, great sense of humor, all of that rolled up with talent to boot. We had the best hopes for her future." Pausing to clear the knot in her throat, she trudged on with a stubborn lift of her chin. "I was there the night she disappeared. My ex-husband and I were at my parents' house for dinner. We were getting ready to leave and I asked my Mum what time she was expected home, because it wasn't like Emily to be late. When she called the parents that drove Em home from the game she'd cheered at, they said they'd dropped her off a half hour earlier. I knew before we found signs of a struggle that I'd never see her alive again. A house full of highly trained agents and he took her right out from under our noses, Lyn."

Lyn interjected in a curious tone, scribbling notes on the pad on her desk. "Your ex-husband? Was he an ex at the time, or is that something else this case is responsible for?"

Too many hours had been spent analyzing that very question, and while it had a bearing on the outcome, Roni could not lay blame where it didn't belong. "It didn't help matters any; but regardless, I got married too young and the relationship wasn't strong enough to survive."

Not wanting to get too off track, Lyn steered her thoughts back to the subject at hand, her voice sounding more preoccupied than she actually was. "Sorry to hear that. You said Emily was cheering at a game? I didn't know they had cheerleaders in England."

Roni's smile was full of sadness as she thought of her sister's happiness in competing. "Yes, since 1982 when American football was adopted as a sport."

Lyn looked up at her with a raised brow, pushing their conversation forward. "Huh, learn something new every day. What other activities was she involved in? Did she take dance, singing lessons?"

Roni nodded as she began to move about again. She didn't like talking about Emily on a personal level, because she didn't want anyone to see the pain she carried. But even as hard as she tried, her body language spoke volumes to Lyn. "Yes, she was involved with everything at one time or another. Though my parents limited her extra activities so she could keep up her grades, she took piano for about five years, and she was really quite fabulous. I remember being surprised that she quit. Her teacher always encouraged her to pursue her talent, but I think she was bored with it. Being a cheerleader was more important at fifteen."

Lyn sat forward, her eyes focusing on a remark on Angela Morris's case file. On her weekly schedule she had piano lessons penciled in on Tuesdays and Thursdays. "Roni, do you remember anything about her teacher? Were they employed through the school system or did your parents hire them privately?"

Roni shook her head as she turned and locked eyes with Lyn, her voice suddenly tired. "I don't know, but I can find out. Why?"

Lyn shook her head absently as she shrugged. "Just something I'd like to check out. Angela Morris took piano lessons on Tuesdays and Thursdays."

Roni tugged at her lip, her brows furrowed in deep thought. "Emily quit her lessons about three weeks before it happened. She was away at cheerleader camp for a week. After she returned, I don't know. Could he have been angry she quit her lessons for something he felt was trivial, wasted talent?"

Finding even the smallest common link had Lyn's thoughts going crazy. She needed to back up and think things through, and she knew she had to do it alone. "Let's just check out the other victims first. This could be a coincidence, so let's see if we really have a lead before we get too excited."

Feeling a little drained, Roni was ready to escape and jumped on the opportunity as she nodded and returned to the sofa to gather her things. "Yeah, I'll get with Ty and start making some inquiries. We were going to start on the customs trace to see if there have been any personal horticulture claims, anyway."

Lyn nodded absently, her thoughts already diverted elsewhere. "That's a good idea. We'll pick this up later, okay?"

Roni could only hope her strangled reply sounded somewhat affirmative as she left Lyn's office, her first priority to find a quiet place in which to regroup her thoughts.

*   *   *   *

By seven that evening Roni felt as if she'd go cross-eyed if she stared at the computer screen for one more minute. Sighing loudly, she slouched backwards and covered her face, jumping when strong hands gripped her shoulders. Opening her eyes she smiled into Dean's face, her voice low. "You scared the hell out of me. I thought it was hands off in the office."

Dean leaned down with a grin, his lips a breath from her ear when he whispered, "Then let's get out here and go get something to eat. I'm starving."

She laughed as he pulled her from the chair, his boyish grin charming her completely. "Does your stomach always come first, Colby?"

He released her hand as they neared the corridor. He was never careless when it came to pissing Mason off. "It depends what's on the menu, Donavan. Come on, I'd like to take you somewhere nice."

The tightness in her shoulders intensified at the thought of sitting in a fancy restaurant, and Roni gave him her sweetest smile as she pulled on her jacket. "Wouldn't you rather grab a sandwich and go a few rounds at Pops? I could stand to work off some of this tension."

Dean's laughter filled the elevator as the doors closed and she turned to give him a look full of innocence. "What?"

He shook his head and wondered at his dumb luck. Of course his perfect woman would live on the wrong side of the world. "You're not playing fair. I think you're trying to make me fall in love with you."

The elevator doors opened to the garage and she gave him a sly smile as she walked out, her voice heavy with innuendo. "It's not your love I'm after, Cowboy."

Dean watched her walk away and grabbed the elevator door as it started to close. With those hips in that skirt, her intent was obvious, and he shook his head slowly as his pulse quickened. "You're bad, Donavan, so, so bad." He heard her soft laughter echo through the empty space as he unlocked the door of his truck, keeping an eye on her until she was safe in her rental before he followed.

    *   *   *   *

Dean yawned as he pulled the pager from his belt, his brow furrowing at the message to report to Mason's office immediately. Mason didn't use "immediately" unless he was pissed about something. Leaving his coffee untouched, he made his way to the lion's den, taking a couple of deep breaths to calm his nerves on the way. He was just being paranoid. There was no way Mason could know about him and Roni fooling around. Could he? Passing the glass wall of the plush office, his glance inside was unrevealing as to the nature of Mason's mood. Tapping on the door, he opened it, keeping his tone casual. "You paged me?"

Mason looked at him for a moment in puzzlement, a movement outside his window bringing him to his feet and around his desk. "No, I didn't, but come in."

Dean checked his pager again, watching as Mason opened his door and called out to the passerby. "Dr. Donavan, I'd like to see you."

Excusing herself from her conversation, Roni entered his office, giving Dean the slightest of looks before she turned to face Mason. He sat on the edge of his desk and crossed his arms over his chest, and she could tell he was furious. You wouldn't know it from his outward demeanor, but his eyes were sparkling like glass and her gut tightened in anticipation.

Already sensing the mood, Dean was trying to back out of the room when Mason glanced his way before leveling Roni with another glare. "Dean, you might as well stay. This will concern you too. Dr. Donavan, would you like to sit down?"

Anxiety knotted in her stomach because she knew what was coming, and she could only wish it was about Dean. She wasn't that lucky. "I think I'll stand. I tend to pace when I get going."

Dean watched her with a casual eye but wondered if she knew she had turned just slightly, facing Mason sidelong as if she were facing an opponent. She was going on the defensive and he was suddenly very curious as to why. Mason was quick to enlighten him.

"You have every right to be nervous, since you're the only person here who may have a clue as to why I'm receiving phone calls from the goddamned Chief of the British Security Service!"

He was nearly shouting when he finished, and Roni took a deep breath before answering, trying to make light of the situation. "I'd say because Finneas Rourke has been calling in favors again."

Mason was so angry with her for putting him in this position he could have strangled her. Her dishonesty was beyond disrespectful, and he had not expected it from her. "You could have told me that Emily Rourke was your sister; or better yet, you could have warned me that your father was involved with the Secret Intelligence Service, Donavan."

Roni's head fell, guilt heavy in her voice as she collected her thoughts. "One mention of MI6 and you wouldn't have invited me."

Even as he felt a twinge of sympathy for her plight, Mason's tone was decisively hard. "Damn straight I wouldn't have. You took advantage of your superior's inexperience with this case, Roni. The Yard cold-cased this investigation before he took over your department, and you manipulated the evidence to gain his cooperation. Neither he nor I would have approved your assistance had we been given full disclosure of the threats against you. Not only that but you've taken it upon yourself to include the confidential files of your sister's murder ..."

Roni's temper snapped, the injustice rising like bile in her throat. "Because that's where they belong. She's part of this investigation, Mason, no matter how much my father would deny it. How many more girls have to die before someone steps out on a limb and does something about it? I can do something, Mason. I have the knowledge, and I won't let his threats stop me. I can help you solve this case."

Mason took a deep breath, shaking his head in disbelief as he interrupted. "Yes, and I've spent the last few hours on a conference call trying to convince everyone involved of that. No one is questioning your abilities, Veronica. On the contrary, I understand that I am in the company of—and I think the exact words were—a treasure of the Crown. But there's your father's position to consider. Your deliberate deception and your lack of protection are his main concerns. However, your sister's files are to be removed from this investigation immediately. That indiscretion you'll have to answer for when you get home."

Roni nodded as her gaze found her shoes, her lack of response prompting Mason to continue. "You understand that your superiors want you off this case and away from this situation …"

Roni's head snapped up, her unhappiness with her father's interference at an all-time high as she nearly groaned out loud. "Please don't send me home, Mason. I know I can help this team."

Mason agreed but held up a hand to stop her plea, his tone still unbending. "I may not approve of your methods, but I do understand your motives. That's the only reason I went to the mat for you to secure your participation. But there's a hitch."

His tone had changed. With one sentence he had gone from boss to protector and her tone turned pleading. "Come on, Mason, don't do it. I don't need protection. I can't work that way."

She fought the compulsion to stomp her foot as he stubbornly shook his head, and she made the mistake of looking to Dean for support. What she found was the icy stare of a pissed-off federal officer. Shit. Good-bye privacy.

Mason was still shaking his head at her audacity as he looked meaningfully at Dean before continuing. "When you step out of this building, Agent Colby will be by your side. You have a couch. Colby's on it. Your phone will be wired and a car will be stationed outside your building at all times. And if there is one, just one threat made against you—if he acknowledges your presence at all—you are on the first flight back to England under military escort if need be. Nonnegotiable. Take it or pack now."

She knew her father. Just as he'd had the Chief of MI5 call today, he would have her marched back to England like a naughty child and scolded for disobeying his wishes. He'd been damned unbearable since Emily's death, and she knew he was already coming unglued to learn she'd released sealed documents about her murder. With no recourse in sight, she sighed and gave Mason a slight shrug. "Anything you say, as long as I can stay and help put an end to this insanity."

Mason had to smile. He had too much Irish blood not to admire her tenacity. "You are my responsibility now, Veronica. I gave my word as to your safety, and I take my word very seriously. Dean, any questions? I want 24/7 armed protection, blanket surveillance. You'll take care of the details?"

Dean nodded. His voice, quiet until now, had an angry edge to it. "I'll take care of it."

Roni looked from one to the other, her response full of sarcasm. "I really don't think all of this drama is necessary."

Mason raised his hand, his tone firm. "That's obvious. But as I said, I'm responsible for you now, and I won't take the threat of a murderer lightly, even if you do. I'll see you both at ten o'clock."

With a clear dismissal Dean turned and opened the door for Roni and was about to close it behind him when Mason spoke again. "Oh, and Colby, you might want to give Dr. Donavan her pager back."

Dean closed the door with an ashen face, pulling his pager from his belt at the same time Roni pulled hers. Flipping it over he saw the number stenciled on the back and muttered a low explicative, silently swapping with Roni before walking away without a backward glance.

*   *   *   *

Lyn found Roni in the small office she was using in the lab, her question full of anger as she stormed into the room. "Mason pulled Emily from the case files and won't tell me why. What the hell is going on?"

Coloring slightly, Roni found herself embarrassed to own up to her deception and repented with naked honesty. "I'm sorry, Lyn. Emily was never supposed to be included in the case files. Because of the discrepancies, it was decided her murder wasn't related, and she was never considered part of Scotland Yard's investigation. And too, because my father is a retired director from MI6, they handled the investigation at a higher level and her files are considered classified. Or they were, before I shared them with you."

Reeling from her admission, Lyn sank into the chair in front of the desk, her shocked tone making Roni smile. "Oh Roni, you could get in so much trouble."

Roni leaned a hip against the desk and shrugged, wishing desperately that she felt as blasé as she sounded. "I'm not anticipating the first call with my father, and I could get suspended if they pushed it; but I needed validation for my beliefs, and I can't get that without evidence." With a sad thought her voice filled with remorse as she added, "Of course, now my credibility has been stained with you guys …"

Lyn dismissed her worries with a wave of her hand, her voice full of confidence. "You don't worry about us. You've already proven your credibility and everyone here considers you part of the family. But still, I don't want to drop Emily's case either. I think it's definitely connected."

Roni had to smile at Lyn's conviction, her voice filling with gratitude as she responded. "Well, so do I, and that's why I went out on the limb to include her case history. All my father's people were concerned with was proving her murder wasn't associated to his position. With that accomplished, they buried her file. And now, once again, Emmy's voice has been silenced."

Although her eyes were bright with mischief, Lyn's expression turned complacent as she rose to leave for their meeting, an underlying emphasis in her voice when she responded. "Emily's voice can still be heard, Roni. We don't need those files with you sharing everything you have stored in that file cabinet of a brain of yours."

Roni's spirit lifted and her soft laughter lingered in the empty space as she followed Lyn to the elevator. "No, I guess we don't, do we?"

CHAPTER 4

▼

Roni rode in silence for what seemed like forever, her only positive thought in that time being that at least she didn't have to drive anymore. She usually ended up a nervous wreck from driving on the wrong side of the road, so she was glad to turn the driving over to Dean, even if he wasn't speaking to her right now. He hadn't spoken to her since they had left Mason's office, and it was only after it was obvious he wasn't going to her apartment that curiosity finally made her inquire about their destination. "Where are we going?"

Dean barely glanced at her before he diverted his gaze, the edge still in his voice. "To my apartment, so I can pack."

Roni stared at his profile for a second before turning away to look out the window with a heavy sigh. "I'm sorry you got stuck being my nanny. I didn't mean for any of this to happen …"

Dean looked at her disbelievingly, his tone skeptical. "You think I'm pissed because Mason chose me to protect you? Hell, I'm the only one Mason would choose. I'm pissed because you didn't tell me this freak had threatened you, Roni. He could be tracking your movements just as you tracked his. He could be watching you, or worse, you could be dead right now. How can you not take this seriously after what you've seen him do?"

Roni's tone suggested her answer was only logical. "Because killing me wouldn't give him what he craves. I'm not his type. He sent notes to scare me off because the press was giving me the attention he thought he deserved."

Dean pulled the truck into his parking garage, switching off the engine before he turned in the seat to look at her. "And don't you think if he finds out you're here, helping with the case and sharing what you know, that just maybe he won't give a shit about his type?"

Any response she could have come up with was left unsaid as he angrily got out of the truck, snatched her from the passenger side, and slammed the door.

The true depth of his aggravation didn't become evident until they entered his apartment and he impulsively slammed a fist into the kick bag hanging in his living room on his way to his room to pack.

Roni's brow rose at the force behind his punch, her retort full of jest as she leaned against the doorframe of his bedroom. "Wow, and here I thought you weren't holding back on me."

She almost stepped backward from the look she received, his harsh retort hitting her close to her ego. "You have the right to be confident, not delusional. If a man wanted to hurt you, Roni, nothing you've been trained for would stop him; and unbalanced people will do anything to keep from getting caught. Don't confuse bravery with stupidity."

Biting her lip she merely nodded at him before retreating to the living room, her experiences with the men in her family having taught her enough to know to leave him alone for a bit. He would settle down eventually, she hoped.

$$*\qquad*\qquad*\qquad*$$

Roni left Dean to his pouting until they got to her apartment. His demeanor was all business as he came in, deposited his bag, and started checking all of the windows and doors. Kicking off her heels she went into the bedroom to change, Dean's voice cutting into her thoughts from the doorway. "The crew will be here to wire the phone in about twenty minutes."

Roni pulled a worn tee shirt over her head and walked over to stand in front of him, her brow raised in question as she faced his anger. "How long are you going to act like this?"

Dean loosened his tie, his sigh heavy with exasperation. "Until you stop treating me like a stranger and sit down and tell me what I need to know."

Roni nodded at his bluntness. She at least owed him answers. After all, she was sharing more with him than just this case. Somewhere in between the laughs and late night talks they had found an intimacy that went deeper than sex, and her tone was at ease when she answered. "I've got to call my father before they tap the phones. If you can wait, I'll tell you what I can after they leave."

Dean nodded, scratching his chin as he gave her a questioning look. "Uh, where do you want me, stuff wise?"

Roni grinned at his light blush, picking up the phone and dialing the familiar number. "Well, if anyone asks, I'll tell them you're on the couch. But seeing that we've slept together for the last week, I see no reason to stop now. After all, you'd definitely be close enough to protect me in here."

Roni held up a hand and turned towards the window as the phone connected, her tone softening as soon as she heard her mother's voice. "Hey, Mum, it's me. How's things?"

Roni smiled at her tired sigh as Lillian responded, "Hello, love. Same old thing here. The man's come home in a foul mood, your brothers have half the rugby team in the rec room, and I miss you terribly. How's the trip going?"

Roni cleared her throat, her voice still a little shaky as she confessed to her lies. Leave it to her father to make her do her own dirty work. "I wasn't completely honest with you, Mum. I'm in the States working on a case. But I've found Emily's killer and I'm pursuing him. Thought you might as well know why Da is in a mood."

She heard the scrape of a kitchen chair as her mother sat down and felt guilty when she noticed her mum's breathing was uneven. "Lord almighty, Veronica Swade, give a woman some notice before springing something like that on her. I thought your father told you to leave well enough alone when they closed that investigation."

Roni's chin jutted out just a hair as her tone grew a little stronger. "And I promised you I wouldn't stop until I put him away. They have a really good team here and I know we can catch him this time, Mum. I just know it."

A deep sigh and a mother's ever-loyal support came back over the line. "No promise is worth your safety, Veronica, but I know if anyone can catch him, it's you. I also know it's useless to ask you to come home, so please, please, sweetheart, be careful."

Roni took a steadying breath as tears stung her eyes, her response chokingly given. "I will, Mum, I promise. I'm sorry you have to deal with Da's mood."

Lillian scoffed at her concern, her retort full of humor. "You know your father can never stay mad at you very long. Do you want to speak with him?"

Taking a deep breath Roni exhaled slowly, answering with resignation in her voice. "Yes, I might as well get it over with."

Dean walked up behind her and held out a glass of bourbon as he kissed the top of her head, and Roni gave him a small smile as he turned and went about moving in his things. Her comfort with that thought was frightening enough to make her hand tremble and she could only wonder what was wrong with her. What was it about this man that made her feel like she'd known him forever?

The loud commanding voice of her father brought her back to reality and she nearly spilled the drink she was in the process of sipping. "You have a lot of explaining to do, young lady. How dare you run off to the States to chase the likes of that sorry excuse of a human being? How exactly did you expect me to answer for what you've done? After what I've done to keep your sister's murder low profile, and you go behind my back and release sealed documents? Do you realize you could lose your position, Veronica? Or worse, face charges? I've told you time and again that you need to get on with your life. If he's truly there, then good riddance. Let their authorities handle it and get your arse back home, now!"

Roni paced the floor in front of the bed, her accent heavier with the anger that nearly blinded her. "No, I won't come home ... and their authorities were handling it. But now, thanks to you, they're wasting man power by babysitting me as well. And if anyone were pressing charges against me, I'd already be halfway home by now. How the bloody hell did you find out where I was, anyway? I know Harvey didn't come to you."

The tone of his voice indicated she was being absurd to even ask. "You honestly think you could leave the country and not have a trace on your passport and credit cards? I'm more outraged that it took over a week to find out you were in Colorado, and I'm still considering having Harvey's arse for it."

She could have kicked herself for not thinking about that and her aggravation came across in her tone. "Don't take this out on Harvey. This was my doings and everyone involved should know that."

Finn interjected with a good bit of his own irritation, "Oh, believe me, we know. Harvey's only fault was that he trusted you to present him with all the facts instead of researching the case himself. With his transferring from Brussels you knew that he wouldn't be familiar with the case, and you took full advantage of that, Roni, and that kind of deception isn't like you. You've put yourself right back in the thick of danger ..."

With a heavy sigh Roni interrupted his rant. "Good Lord, you know I can take care of myself, Da. Why did you have to go and make a ruckus when you knew I wouldn't let it go? You didn't raise me to quit, and he's already killed three more girls. How am I supposed to get on with my life knowing firsthand the grief and pain he causes every family he touches?"

After a moment's pause a bit of his steam escaped and he was a little more agreeable as he sighed dramatically. "Oh, Roni, you're such a hardheaded lass. You've let your obsession cloud your judgment, and this time he'll kill you when he gets tired of playing the game. You know damn well he will. I won't bury another daughter in my lifetime. So if you do this, number one, leave Emily's name out of it. Two, stay out of the limelight, and away from the crime scenes. Try to keep clear of the press, and for God's sake, keep your mouth shut."

Roni had expected him to be unreasonable, but now he was being downright unrealistic and she let him know with a good bit of gruff. "You know good and damn well that I can't investigate under lock and key. I'll do my best to keep a low profile, as always, but why do you think I didn't tell you to begin with? If I had told you my plans, you would have had my passport suspended and put me under house arrest."

His threat was quick and she smiled at his bluff. "I'm still tempted to send your brothers to fetch you. Did you tell your mother what you've done?"

Taking a sip of her bourbon, she watched the surveillance team unload their gear from the van downstairs, smiling broadly as the rain began and they had to scramble. "I told her I was here on a possible lead, but I didn't tell her I had included Emily's files. Regardless, she's concerned but supportive, like parents are supposed to be."

She could see his grin, hear it in his voice. "Don't be flip and don't give me cause to change my mind. You know all I have to do is make a phone c…."

Roni laughed at the unnecessary reminder of his clout, her retort full of sarcasm. "Yes, I know. I have plenty of protection though, so stay off the phone, Da. You've done enough for one day."

Hearing the door she hurried him off the phone, her sudden emotional state sending her to the bathroom to compose herself. Roni hated lying to her folks; but worse, she hated the separation anxiety that made her feel so weak. Sometimes she wished she could just forget and go on with her life, but she knew that she wouldn't, not as long as Emily's murderer was out there.

✳   ✳   ✳   ✳

Sitting cross-legged on the couch, Roni glared at the equipment on the end table. She hated being treated like a victim, hated the way it made her feel so helpless. When Dean joined her, he purposely blocked her view, his voice firm as he handed her a freshened glass. "Just quit thinking about it. Forget it's even there …"

Fresh tears stung her eyes as she fought the lump in her throat and looked away, a little vulnerability slipping out in his presence. "You all make that sound so easy, and it's not. At least not for me, especially now that I'm alone and thousands of miles away from everything I've ever known."

Dean pulled her chin around so that she was looking at him. His voice was strong yet tender. "You are not alone."

Pulling his hand away, Roni shook her head, a twinge of resentment in her reply. "I am not your job."

Dean reveled in her confusion when he laughed. He knew her game and he wasn't playing, not this time. "I know what my job entails, and what goes on between us, behind these doors, isn't included. You be as testy as you want, but I don't need your protection from this creep. You don't need to push me away like you did your ex and everyone else you care about to keep me safe."

Roni was stunned by his comment and looked at him blankly as she teetered on being angry. Her response, when it came, was full of natural curiosity. "Is that what I'm doing? You think you know me well enough to make such an assessment. Have you ever taken into consideration that maybe I'm just a bitch?"

Dean laughed as he pulled her into an embrace, his breath close to her ear when he responded. "Yeah, I have, but I like you anyway."

His lips stilled against her hair when she spoke, her soft voice genuinely apologetic. "I'm sorry I wasn't more truthful with you, Dean. I should have warned you …"

His sarcastic snort nearly deafened her. "About which part? Emily being your sister, your being here under manipulated authority, or that you practically created an international situation by sharing classified documents from the MI6?"

Tilting her head, she gave him a lopsided grin as she looked up at him. "All of the above?"

Dean laughed as his arms tightened around her and he kissed her temple. "I think Mason would be a better person to apologize to. After all, it was him you got in hot water with your indiscretion; maybe your father too if he holds a position with MI6."

Roni shook her head, a hint of sullenness creeping into her tone. "Nah, he's retired, but he was a tactical director with the Secret Intelligence Service for over forty years. So needless to say, he still gets anything he wants with a phone call to the right person."

"Ah, and if I recall correctly, MI6 is equivalent to our CIA, right?"

Roni answered with a nod and continued in anticipation of his next question. "And the MI5, or the Security Service, is like your FBI."

Dean's brow rose as he looked down at her speculatively. "So why aren't you working with the Service instead of Scotland Yard? And don't tell me you weren't approached, because I won't believe it."

Roni had been approached, several times, and she surprised herself by answering him truthfully. "Because my ex-husband worked for MI5 before he was promoted; and with his friends in the SS and my father's friends in the SIS, I rather wanted to stay at the Yard with my friends. Besides, being at the Yard puts me on street level where I'm more of an asset."

The solid confidence in Dean's soft voice made her blush as he complimented her. "Honey, your skills are an asset on any level."

She chuckled as he lowered his head to nuzzle her neck, her retort full of sarcasm. "Yeah, but I think you're just trying to get in my pants."

His breath was warm against her skin as he laughed, his eyes full of mischief as he gave her a chagrined look. "Damn, I'm busted. So how is it that an Irishman became so entrenched in the SIS anyway?"

Roni shrugged slightly, her voice softening as she discussed her family. "My mother, I guess. My father attended Oxford on scholarship. That's where he met Mum. They wed after graduation and Da stayed in England to enlist in the RAF. Shortly after, he finagled a commission in Dublin until I finished high school. Then we moved back to England so I could attend University."

Dean held up a hand, his tone unbelieving, "Hold up. Don't tell me he moved the whole family to England because you were going to college."

Roni gave him a look like he'd lost his mind. "Of course not. It was always their plan to move back to England when I was ready for Oxford so Mum could be close to her family for a while. I could tell that Da didn't care for the fact that Emily was so young when we moved to the city, probably because he knew he'd lose all control over her upbringing, and he was so right. Mum's family had already picked her school, actually signed her up for activities and practically had her friends picked out for her. The bad part was that she became the focus of Mum's life for eight years, and when it happened, it took us over a month to get her out of the house."

Dean gently pulled a lock of her hair through his fingers, his voice softening as he steered her from the deep side of the conversation. "Are your brothers in the family business too?"

Roni grinned at the thought of them, her handsome, crazy brothers. "Nah, they're big, dumb firemen. All they want to do is play rugby, drink ale, and chase women."

Dean's brow shot up in thought, his smile broadening as he responded. "Sounds like a good life to me."

She rolled her eyes and gave him an unladylike snort. "Yeah, it would. So when do we get to talk about you, anyway?"

Dean grinned, his tone placating as he shrugged. "What do you want to know?"

Roni glanced up at him, her eyes full of curiosity. "You're a handsome, successful guy. Why aren't you married?"

Dean's grin deepened, his voice soft when he looked down at her with a raised brow. "Who say's I'm not?"

He laughed when she jerked away from him with an outraged gasp. His hands were gentle as he tried to pull her back against him. "Jesus, what a look! I'm kidding." When she resisted, his tone sobered, his voice filling with sincerity. "I've never come close to getting married, I swear."

Even as her lips started forming the w, he answered her with a shrug. "I don't know why. I guess because I've never met anyone that was more important to me than my job, or more exciting. Now let's get back on track. You joined the Violent Crimes Division ..."

Roni sighed heavily as she relaxed against him, rattling off a summary of her life so she could get back to his. "And the press found out about my theories, printed them, then he sent me a few letters, the killings stopped there, started here, and now here we are. Bloody hell, what was that?"

They both jumped at the vibration that tickled between them and Dean reached for his belt with a chuckle. "My pager."

His grin quickly disappeared as he read the message, relaying it to Roni even as her pager on the counter began to sound. "We've got another victim. Better get your stuff together."

Roni was off the couch before he finished his sentence, and he wasn't surprised that they were out the door within five minutes.

$$ * \quad * \quad * \quad * $$

Dean squinted into headlights as Mason pulled up in his truck and checked the whereabouts of the team before walking over to greet him. "Hey. Lyn, Juni, and Roni are already here. The police department is standing by, mostly for crowd control."

Mason surveyed the dark alley, the blue lights bouncing off the buildings, creating an eerie strobe effect with the crowds hovering around. Sighing heavily there was a private tone in his voice that not many were privy too "I told Lyn we were running out of time, I want to talk to the first one on the scene, and see if you can get them to move these people back some more. We don't need all this commotion while we're trying to investigate."

Dean nodded and took two steps before Mason stopped him with an angry voice. "I thought you said the scene was clear."

Dean's brow furrowed as he stepped forward to look where Mason was pointing. He knew damn well there hadn't been anyone else in that alley, and his laughter was barely held in check when he realized Mason didn't recognize Roni, not that he blamed him. She cut a totally different figure with her hair down and dressed in jeans and a tee shirt. "That's Donavan, Mason. You might not recognize her without her glasses on."

Mason looked back at her for a instant and then gave Dean a knowing look, his head shaking slowly as he grinned. "Yeah, that must be it. You be smart with that one, Colby. You get what I'm saying?"

Dean just smiled and shook his head as he walked away, his parting words making Mason chuckle. "Sooo too late ..."

*   *   *   *

Roni tucked a strand of hair behind her ear as she jotted down the rest of her thoughts, stowing her note pad in her bag and pulling out her camera. She knew the department would take pictures, but she wanted her own for ready reference. Hearing Dean's voice rising in frustration, she turned towards him to see him and some other agents pushing back the humming crowd. Without thought she raised her camera and took some pictures of the crowd, hoping she could pick up some faces, maybe something out of the ordinary, anything.

She turned at the sound of Mason's voice to see him squat beside Juni next to the body. "What kind of flowers are these?"

Roni glanced at the bouquet placed so delicately between the girl's hands, her voice soft when she answered his question. "Phlox, August. Tell Ty to focus on missing persons reports filed on white females, sixteen to seventeen years of age, with an August birth date. It won't take long for a name."

Mason nodded as he studied the wounds on the body, his eyes full of sadness when he looked at Roni. "I don't know how you do it, how you keep going ..."

Roni dismissed the twinge of admiration in his voice, keeping her own carefully schooled. "The same as everyone else in this field: we're trained to block out our personal feelings, to turn a situation like this into forensics and evidence to catch the person responsible." Sharing a knowing look with Juni, her smile was void of humor when she spoke on a more personal level. "That doesn't mean we don't all have our bad days."

Mason gave her shoulder a pat as he addressed Juni. "Speaking of evidence, I think it's time we get her to the lab and take a better look."

Juni nodded as she gently removed the flowers with a gloved hand and placed them in a protective bag. "I'll be finished in a few. I've had my fill of this alley."

With a simple nod Mason left her to work, looking to Lyn to shed some insight on what drives someone to do something so gruesome to a girl so young. "Hey, kiddo, getting anything?"

Lyn gave him a sad smile as he walked up, wishing she had more for him as she motioned around the alley and shook her head. "This is a drop site, not a crime scene, just like our other three. Why is he putting them in the middle of downtown?"

Mason squeezed her shoulder and gave her a small reassuring smile, sharing her frustration but unwilling to voice it. "We'll get there, don't worry."

*   *   *   *

Juni opened the lab door, stifling a yawn as she stopped and handed Dean a cup of coffee. "Maybe you should go home and get some sleep."

Nodding towards Roni hard at work in the examination room, he gently blew on the hot brew. "I go home when she does."

Juni watched her for a few seconds. Her precise procedures and her thoroughness were true signs of a perfectionist, and Juni couldn't help but think that Roni reminded her of herself at that age. "You might want to stretch out then, because you may be here a while. She looks like she could go all night."

Juni didn't know who blushed first, but she quickly retreated to the workroom, giving Roni a smile as she finished her notes into her handheld recorder. "Are you satisfied yet?"

Roni took a deep breath and exhaled slowly, her hand absently reaching up to push her glasses up. "Strangled unconscious, two stab wounds to the heart and lungs. Betcha a bottle of Irish whiskey the weapon will be an eight-inch, serrated hunting blade."

Juni looked at her with deep regret, her hand resting on her chest. "I wish I had a chance at that wager, because I bet you could get your hands on some really good Irish whiskey."

Roni smiled softly, her voice filling with warmth. "My Da has a bottle of whiskey in his office that he swears was brewed by leprechauns themselves. My mum, of course, says it's a bottle of McGregor's worth about $5000. I wouldn't know, because I haven't been able to get my hands on it."

Juni laughed as she shook her head in disbelief. "That's okay. We'll settle for the next to the really good stuff and save a few pennies. Are you really gonna make that big oaf fall out of that chair out there? We know what happened to her and she'll be here in the morning. Take a break and get some sleep, Roni. I know it has been a tough day for you, and now it's 2:00 AM and it's only gotten worse."

Roni rubbed her forehead, her agenda still forming in her mind. "I dunno, Juni. I still want to sweep the body for prints …"

Juni's exasperated sigh cut her off. "If there are any, which I doubt, they will still be there in the morning. We have these really neat chemicals and special lights we use …"

Rolling her eyes Roni gave into her ribbing, giving her a little of her own as she shrugged out of her lab coat. "Okay, okay, you win. I can tell you get cranky when you're up past your bedtime, so we'll start fresh in the morning."

CHAPTER 5

▼

Roni paced the section of carpet beside her chair with her eyes trained on the large wall screen, and her ear tuned into Lyn's thoughts. Time was ticking away and their slow progress was making her even more anxious because she knew the longer they took, the closer he would come to another victim. The map grid she was studying had pinpoint dots representing the drop sites of all of their victims, and something about the pattern was beginning to look familiar to her. That it was familiar was strange in itself, but as a visitor to the city she had been staring at a map of downtown for weeks, and with a squint of her eye, she leaned over Tyler's shoulder, her request quietly voiced. "Could you add this building to the grid, please?"

With a small nod and a few keystrokes, a blue dot appeared right where she knew it would: dead center in the middle of the drop sites. "Here's why your victims are being dropped in downtown Denver."

Lyn stopped mid sentence, her expression puzzled as she looked up at Roni. "What?"

Roni pointed at the screen on the wall, her tone matter-of-fact. "Your victims. The other night you asked why he was dropping them in downtown. They're not being dropped, more like delivered—to us." Pointing to the blue dot, she looked at Mason for emphasis. "That's us. The drop sites are beginning to circle the building."

With a sudden thought she looked to Tyler, her face full of curious exploration. "Ty, can you pull up the victims' addresses and grid them for us on an area map?"

The keystrokes grew faster, and Roni looked at Lyn with a shrug. "Doesn't hurt to check. Are you sure it's a no go on the piano teacher?"

Lyn smiled and gave her an animated nod. "'Fraid so. Only four took piano and all from different people, two of whom were women. Do you have a theory on why the pattern? Or are you working on a hunch?"

Roni looked back to the screen, twisting her glasses in her fingers as she nodded. "No theory, just a hunch."

Mason cleared his throat as the grid popped up. "Pretty good hunch, Donavan."

The four victims' addresses patterned out a duplicate grid of their inner-city zone, and Roni spoke out loud more to voice her thoughts than anything. "All of the girls have different addresses but come from the same vicinity? Ty, what's the center point of their grid?"

"A little town called Castle Rock. It's about thirty miles from here."

Roni stopped, stared up at the screen, and then shrugged to the group, her mind a blank. "Okay, that's all I've got."

Lyn sat forward with a grin, her voice dripping with sarcasm and her eyes full of laughter. "You sure you don't want to go ahead and solve the case? You seem to be on a roll."

Roni gave her a grin and took her seat, her head shaking slowly. "No, I don't know why he would choose girls from thirty miles from here. It seems to me it would be easier to kill a girl in the city than to drag one from the suburbs. Unless, that is, these four girls share something in common that the other six don't, but we already know that none of them attended the same schools or churches."

All eyes turned toward Dean as he entered the room, his cell to his ear, his voice full of command as he gave orders to the person on the other end. Hanging up, he gave Mason a look of resignation. "He's broken pattern. We have another victim."

Lyn looked at Roni, her eyes full of alarm. "He's never killed again so soon."

Roni stuffed her files in her notebook in disdain. "He killed four girls then broke pattern when he killed Emily two days after a victim. Now after four more girls, he breaks pattern again. Isn't that a pattern within itself?"

Counting it up in her head, Lyn nodded in agreement, her sigh heavy as she gathered her things. "Yes, it could be."

Mason stood with a deep sigh, motioning to Roni to sit back down. "Sorry, kiddo, you have to stay here. Too much daylight." Roni gave him a disbelieving look, her words cut short by his brief reminder. "My call, Donavan, remember?

Spend the time working with Tyler to find a connection between these girls. We'll be back soon enough."

Not wanting to risk deportation, she bit her tongue and gave him a curt nod as she sat down and watched them leave, throwing Tyler a glare when he chuckled. "What?"

Shaking his head he continued to scan the information popping up on his screen, a bit of chiding in his voice. "I'm just wondering if I look that forlorn every time I'm left behind."

Roni sighed heavily and tried to turn her attention to the project at hand. "I just don't like being put on a leash. But, on the bright side, between the two of us and our genius, I'm sure we can find something to dazzle Mason with."

Tyler looked up from his monitor, his grin full of confidence. "Well, so far two of the four American victims were born at Castle Rock Memorial. How's that for genius?"

Roni abandoned her own laptop to go sit beside him, her interest instantly piqued. "Bloody brilliant. He could work there, could pick his victims from patient records."

✳   ✳   ✳   ✳

By the time the team returned, she and Tyler had confirmed that all four American victims had been born at the same hospital and had started a program to scan hospital employment records and select anyone fitting their profile. Of course, that was only after making a pact not to tell how they accessed the records without a court order, because some things, for the sake of justice, were best kept between two junior hackers. With Tyler searching the missing persons' data bank for their newest victim, Roni hopped the elevator to the basement to meet the team at the back door. Juni was the first one inside, and from the expression she wore, Roni knew instantly that something was wrong. "What is it, Juni?"

Juni lowered her head, keeping her voice quiet as she steered Roni to the lab. "There's something written on the body. I can't read it, but Mason's convinced it's got something to do with you being at that crime scene the other night."

Roni had absently started rubbing her stomach as Juni spoke, the intense knotting of anxiety gnawing at her insides. "It probably does. How long before she gets here?"

Juni hung up her jacket and put on her lab coat, glancing at the wall clock as she did. "About five minutes. You okay? You look pale."

Roni waved her off, her voice weak. "It's sickening to think he may have killed a girl solely to send me a message, Juni. Where are the flowers?"

As if on cue, an agent opened the door to deliver the evidence, leaving Juni to raise a brow at Roni. "That was spooky. I think they are Daylilies. That's October, right?"

Roni's smile was sad as she looked at the flowers, giving Juni a wink as she confirmed her assumption. "You have been paying attention. Yes, on all accounts. I'll call Ty and tell him to limit the search to girls born in October."

Leaving the room to make the call, Roni waited until the orderlies left before returning to eye the corpse with a wary glance. "Okay, where is it?"

Juni crooked her finger, motioning for Roni to approach from her side of the table. "Help me turn her. It's on her back."

With shaking hands Roni helped with the task, her anxiety only increasing when she finally got a good look at the strange words written on the girl's skin. The message, "Я знал, что Вы придете домой ко мне," was confusing; but nevertheless, she was positive it was meant for her.

Juni looked at her suspiciously as she returned with a swab to test the red substance he'd used to write with. "Are you sure you're okay?"

Roni looked at her with glazed over eyes, her voice barely a whisper. "It's a marker, Juni. He wanted to be sure I could read it."

Juni's hands froze and she looked at Roni curiously and asked softly, "And can you?"

Roni's eyes grew bright with unshed tears as she nodded, answering with a shaky voice. "Yes, it's Russian, and it says, 'I knew you'd come home to me.'"

Juni gave her an understanding smile as her eyes filled with compassion. "I'm sorry. I know you were trying to keep a low profile. It sucks considering you were only at one crime scene."

Roni's head jerked up and she snapped her fingers, causing Juni to jump. "Geez, what?"

Roni was already headed for her backpack she kept thrown in the corner of the lab. "You're right. I was at only one crime scene, and I took pictures of the crowd the other night."

When she stood and turned, she was looking into Dean's questioning gaze as he walked in on the conversation. "And the pictures might tell you what? And be straight with me, Roni."

Roni rolled her eyes at him, walking back into the exam room as she rewound her film. "If they saw me, then maybe they're in the pictures I took at the scene. Jeez, one little discrepancy and you treat me like a criminal? This is the first time he has written in a foreign language, meaning he didn't intend for just anyone to read it. Do either of you know if Mason recognized it?"

Dean looked over the strange letters scrawled on the victim and got a little angrier, his eyes bright with it as he leveled her with an unwavering look. "What's it say, Donavan?"

Roni noticed Juni quietly disappearing from the room, which meant the protective edge in Dean's voice hadn't been obvious only to her. "You can't go nuts over this, Dean. I really need you to stay focused and help me find this guy."

She wasn't surprised that the edge in his voice hadn't dissipated one bit. "You tell me what it says or I'll go find a translator myself."

Studying him for a minute, she sighed heavily, reading the phrase in Russian, then translating. "I knew you'd come home to me."

Dean's brows furrowed together and he gave her a questioning look as he asked the question plaguing her mind. "What the hell does that mean?"

Roni chewed on her lip, her head shaking slowly. "I don't know."

With an exasperated sigh he ran a hand over his face, preparing for the long evening of work he was sure was about to commence. "That's just what we need, another twist to this fiasco."

Roni gave him a pat on the back, her eyes taking on a seductive gleam as she steered his thoughts elsewhere. "Well, speaking of twists, how 'bout you show me where the dark room is and help me develop this film?"

Dean laughed softly as his hand fell to the small of her back to steer her from the room. "I actually don't know where it is, but we can get lost looking for it together."

Resisting a giggle, Roni fell in step with an easy grin. "Sounds like a good plan, and you never answered my question by the way."

"Which was?"

Rolling her eyes, Roni glared at him as she sighed dramatically. "I asked you if Mason knew …"

Both stopped when the elevator doors opened a few feet away, the look on Mason's face making Dean's sarcastic response unnecessary. "Yep, I think he knows."

Mason stormed toward them with an angry stride and an angrier tone, shaking the Polaroid picture in his hand at Roni. She should have known he'd find his own translator for sure. "You are not coming over here and putting my team and my city at more risk by enraging a serial killer. I told you if he acknowledged …"

"And by acknowledging my presence he gave us another part of the puzzle, Mason. I'm the only person here that can figure out what this message means.

I'm telling you that he has not broken pattern. Unless we catch him, the next girl will show up again in six weeks. The next, six weeks after ..."

Weighing his dilemma, Mason muttered an oath and addressed Dean in a commanding voice. "This doesn't leave the team, and I don't want to see her for at least 48 hours." When Roni started to interrupt, he leveled her with such a look that she clamped her mouth shut, and he proceeded with his instructions to Dean. "I don't care where you take her, just get her out of Denver until I can get this frenzy under control. I've not only got the mayor and police commissioner on my ass, I've got the press all over me, and the last thing I need is for them to discover he's writing notes on the bodies."

"I'm sorry, Mason ..." Even though Roni's tone was apologetic, Mason cut her off with a hand before abruptly turning back toward the elevator.

"Two days, Donavan."

With her safety in question there was only one destination in mind and as Dean watched Mason storm back off, he sighed heavily, not anticipating the drive ahead. Glancing down at Roni, his comment was forgotten when he saw the forlorn expression on her face, his retort full of laughter. "Christ, Donavan, I've never seen anyone look so miserable to have the weekend off."

*   *   *   *

Pulling up to the ranch-styled home, Dean turned off the motor and reached over to gently shake Roni awake, his tone preoccupied as he moved to get out of the SUV. "I'm going in to let them know we're here. I'll be right back."

Roni stifled a yawn and nodded as she tried to get her bearings, a task she was finding difficult considering that it had grown dark during her nap and she had no idea where she was. Looking out the window, she watched Dean jog up the stairs to the wood and stone veranda, his pace unfaltering as he walked into the house brimming with life.

The smells emitting from the porch sent Dean straight to the kitchen, and he entered with a broad smile for his brother-in-law as he rose from his seat at the table, his hand outstretched in greeting. "Man, you're just in time."

Dean shook Jason's hand, his attention drawn to the toddler happily playing in what looked to be a mixture of peas and carrots. "I don't know. It looks like Griffin here is taking care of business for me. Damn, he's gotten big."

Jason laughed as he returned to his chore of feeding his youngest of three, his voice full of pride. "He won't shy away from a meal, that's for sure."

Feeling the hand on his back, Dean turned as his sister leaned around him to set a bowl on the table, her sarcastic remark nothing more than what he'd expect from his older sibling. "Just think, the next time you see him, he'll be walking."

Dean grabbed her as she turned away, his retort full of amusement as she tried to pull away from his embrace. "Oh, sis, if I was out here every weekend, you'd just gripe because I was in your way."

Carol's short laugh was sarcastic as she disentangled herself, her rebuff for him full of jest as she went to call the kids down for dinner. "Yeah, well, we'd like the opportunity nonetheless. Get washed up to eat."

Dean hated to decline the offer, but he wasn't subjecting Roni to the chaos that was about to ensue. "I'm not staying. Roni's out in the truck and I just stopped in to let you know we were here."

Jason knew the look Dean got all too well, and he sighed heavily as he arose from the table, his wife's rant on her brother just another source of noise as his other two children descended from the back stairs to excitedly greet their uncle. There was no way Dean was getting out of the house without dinner, and knowing what had to be done, Jason took matters into his own hands, returning moments later with Roni by his side.

Roni had been taken aback when he had come to get her, but the scene in front of her was one she reveled in. She wouldn't have thought Dean could be rattled, but holding an argument with his sister while being asked three hundred questions by the two teenagers hanging on him was beginning to take its toll, and she could only chuckle at his discomfort.

Jason smiled as she laughed softly beside him, his voice full of warmth as they watched the assault in front of them. "Can't you tell there's a lot of love in this house?"

Although Jason had said it jokingly, Roni's response was void of humor, the sincerity in her tone giving him a second's pause. "Yes, I can."

Letting out a shrill whistle, Jason grinned as Griffin mimicked the noise, his eyes coming to rest knowingly on his wife as everyone froze and looked at them in shock. "Roni's here. Can we eat now?"

Dean nearly groaned at the look that possessed his sister's eyes, his low warning unheard by the woman he addressed. "Don't even start, Carol."

Carol's smile was brilliant as she ignored her brother and moved forward to meet the beautiful woman standing beside her husband, a newfound hope in her heart for the death of Dean's bachelorhood. "What a mess to walk into. Hi, I'm Carol, Dean's sister. You met my husband, Jason, and this is our daughter, Stephanie, and our sons, Matt and Griffin ..."

"Welcome to Bedlam."

Carol swatted Dean with a dishtowel, her voice full of amusement as she returned to the kitchen. "You hush. Make yourself at home, Roni. Dinner will be on in five if you guys would like to freshen up."

It was an offer they were both quick to take her up on and it was a few minutes later that Roni found herself in the broad hallway outside the bath, her natural curiosity drawing her to the near gallery-sized collection of frames lining the wall. A history of pictures told her that this was more than Dean's sister's house. It was Dean's childhood home and it was a place of happiness and love. It also told her loads about the man she'd been so intimate with the last few weeks. His voice cut into her thoughts as he walked up behind her, his words bringing a smile to her lips. "What are you frowning for? You're not in any of them."

Roni comfortably received his embrace as he pulled her against his chest, his lips on her neck making her response a bit breathless. "I was just thinking I should be ashamed for all that I don't know about you."

Dean's breath was warm in her ear as he chuckled, his soft words making her cheeks flame with color. "I'd think you'd be more ashamed for the things you do know about me."

Ignoring his innuendo, Roni instead commented on the numerous certificates scattered throughout the collage of portraits. "Honor Society, high school football hero, Colorado State MVP, two-time All American, and top of your class at the Academy. So do you make apple pie too?"

When he nipped her earlobe she jerked away from him, her stern warning not quite extinguishing the flare of mischief in her eyes. "That'll be enough of that, Mr. All American. I'm not finished. There's this nice shot of you as a young lad, circa 1970 something …"

Her teasing smile ignited a desire in Dean that demanded satisfaction and Roni was cut short when he roughly pulled her back into his arms, his sudden kiss so full of passion that it was impossible not to respond to him, no matter where they were.

A clearing of the throat behind them hit Roni like a bucket of water and she was quicker to react, pushing Dean away and leaving him a little dazed when he turned to see his niece standing there looking at them like a hall monitor.

Stephanie's tone was full of sass as she crossed her arms over her chest and lifted a well-arched brow at him, her sapphire blue eyes sparkling with amusement. "Well, if this is business, I'd sure hate to see what you do for pleasure. Mom said to come eat before it gets cold, but I guess I can tell her that's not a problem …"

Ignoring the embarrassment burning his face, Dean gave her a stern look, the teasing lilt of his voice a direct contrast to the glare she received. "You don't need to tell her jack. Jesus, don't you have some Barbie dolls or something to play with? How old are you now?"

Stephanie gave him her best smile, her saccharine sweet retort flung over her shoulder as she turned back toward the kitchen. "I'm fifteen and, unlike you, I quit playing with Barbie dolls a long time ago."

Roni stepped around him when he stalled from shock, her grin broad as she passed. "Ohhh, I like her."

*   *   *   *

The hospitality and camaraderie within Dean's family had Roni easily feeling like one of the clan, and it was with great regret that she walked onto the veranda later in the evening and straight into the men's conversation. The underlying concern in Jason's voice hit her close to heart and she felt a moment's guilt for his worry. "I talked to Bill and we'll be running a live perimeter patrol all weekend. We'll have constant armed riders on the fences and teams at all four entrances of the ranch, but I'm still not sure if I'm alright with all of this …"

Dean was quick to put his brother-in-law at ease, his hand falling to the man's shoulder as a sign of reassurance. "Jay, you know I wouldn't bring her here if there was even the remotest chance it put your family in danger. The extra patrols are nothing but precautionary, just to be on the safe side."

Jason nodded absently as he exhaled slowly and flipped the butt of his cigarette into the darkness, his voice void of conviction as dark thoughts swirled in his brain. "Yeah, well, I hope so."

Taking a deep breath, Roni pushed the unpleasantness to the rear and attempted to make a little more noise as she rounded the corner of the veranda, her casual tone an effort with tears that clogged her throat. "So this is where you two got off to."

Dean turned with a welcoming smile, his voice light as he held out a hand for her. "Yep, here we are. Did you finally get Stephanie's 101 questions answered?"

Roni had spent the last thirty minutes giving in to Stephanie's inquisitiveness and still wasn't sure she'd quenched a fraction of the teenager's curiosity. "I don't know. I left her touring Ireland via the Internet, but I only escaped with the promise that we'd come watch her run barrels tomorrow. She's very excited that you're here."

Dean looked at Jason inquisitively and he answered the unasked question without pause. "County Arena in town. Tomorrow's state semi-finals."

Dean muttered an oath as he wrestled with the decision of whether or not to go, almost relieved when the choice was made for him with Roni's quiet words. "You're the one who told everyone we were here for a breather. If we don't go then they'll think we're in hiding, and you know he would never challenge you here."

Sighing heavily Dean absently rubbed her back as he looked out at the inky outline of the Colorado Rockies, his reply sounding stronger than he felt. "I know he won't."

Pushing away from a post, Jason gave Dean a hearty cuff on the shoulder, a bit of chiding in his farewell as he headed for the house. "Okay, well I guess I'll see you guys in the mornin' then. Carol cleaned the cabin after you called, so I figure you guys have everything you need, but give us a shout if she missed anything."

Dean chuckled as he thought of Carol's obsessive nature, his sarcastic reply called over his shoulder. "When you can't find anything, let me know, because I'm sure we'll have it."

CHAPTER 6

▼

Two miles away from the main house and nestled by the gathering pond of a small waterfall, Roni found herself in front of a small replica and she stepped out of the truck with a broad grin, her voice full of jest as she took her backpack from Dean. "I'm home!"

Dean laughed as he turned an appreciative eye to the view, his response full of pride as he followed her toward the porch. "Yeah, this has been my haven since Dad and I built it when I was sixteen. Not a bad place to escape to, huh?"

Roni stopped on the second step and turned to face him, disbelief evident in her tone. "You built this?"

Stopping at the foot of the porch, he grinned at the shocked look on her face, his voice filling with sarcasm. "Yeah, and its safe, Donavan …"

Making use of her height advantage, Roni interrupted him with a soft kiss, the sincerity of her compliment warming his cheeks. "Now, I'm impressed."

Dean wrapped an arm around her waist as he stepped closer, his grin turning mischievous as he easily lifted her off her feet. "Aw hell, wait until you get inside then."

Roni laughed as she wriggled from his grasp, her retort full of tease as she headed for the door. "Would it be too much to ask if you have Internet access …?"

Dean grabbed her backpack to stop her, his tone serious when she looked up at him inquisitively. "Take a break, Donavan."

Roni chuckled at his protective tone, her light response unconvincing at best. "I am …"

Dean scoffed at the innocent look she tried to pawn off on him, sarcasm heavy in his response as he playfully pushed her inside. "Yeah, right, you wouldn't know a break if it bit you on the ass.

*   *   *   *

It was a couple hours later that Dean woke with a start, blinking as he sat up on the couch to see Roni dumping her bag out on the floor. "Well, that was a big break. What are you doing?"

She kept digging through the debris before holding up an object in triumph. "Looking for my magnifying glass. You dozed off. Why don't you go to bed?"

Dean raked a hand through his dark hair, squinting at the clock on the fireplace mantle. "Why don't *we* go to bed? You need to get some sleep too, you know."

Roni shook her head as she went back to the kitchen table, her laptop humming in the middle of folders and pictures. "Until I get a good look at these crime scene photos, I will just toss and turn."

Dean stifled a yawn as he squatted to pick her stuff up off the floor. "I should have made you leave all this crap in Denver. I think you're becoming obsessed."

Roni chuckled in response, her reply absently given. "Took you this long?"

He heard her response but his attention was drawn elsewhere. In the pile of junk she carried in her bag there was a stack of pictures held together with a thick rubber band, and Dean could only hope this was his chance for some payback.

Pulling out a chair at the table he sat down and shook the stack of pictures at Roni. "Anything circa 1970's in here?"

Roni laughed when she saw what he held. "Oh-no, there are some really embarrassing family photos in there."

Dean pulled the band off with an exaggerated gesture and gave her a sweet smile. "That's what I'm hoping."

Roni snorted before turning her attention back to her photos. "You've been forewarned, Colby, I'm not responsible for any nightmares you may have."

Dean merely chuckled as he thumbed through the pictures, already knowing who each person was just from Roni's description of them. Flipping to the next picture in the pile his smile disappeared as he sat forward to hold it out for her to look at. "Roni, when was this?"

She glanced up and shook her head at the picture he was holding, her voice full of humor. "My roommate in college talked me into that. Hideous, isn't it?"

Dean gave her an exasperated look, shaking the picture in front of her. "No, look at the picture, Roni. Look at it and tell me when it was, and how long was it like that?"

Roni took the picture she had been ruthlessly teased about, the resemblance between sisters only heightened by her blonde experiment. Seconds into studying her and Emily's faces, her heart bottomed out and she realized what Dean was insinuating. "A year before graduation, and it was only blonde for about three months. I doubt it's of any consequence."

Her tone, so full of disbelief and denial, made Dean smile knowingly. He'd seen too many suspects in cuffs due to Lyn's off-the-wall theories not to consider every hunch. "Three months? It only took me three minutes to fall for you."

She stared at him for a long minute. His gaze was direct and unwavering, and adorable. Her heart was beginning to ache at the thought of leaving him and she gave him a warm smile as she threw the picture back at him. "You mean it only took three minutes for me to knock you on your ass. You're reaching, Dean. Oxford University hosts anywhere up to 18,000 students from over a dozen different colleges. This hasn't anything to do with a couple months of my life when I had blonde hair. I was a bookworm, aside from a couple of student societies. I wasn't anything special."

Dean stretched as another yawn hit him and he slowly rose from the chair. "Whatever, I don't believe that bullshit; but nevertheless, we'll see what Lyn has to say about it Monday. I'm going to bed."

Roni snapped her mouth shut, her eyes trying to burn a hole through his back. "I've never shown pictures of you in polyester pants and an awful Afro. I see no reason to bring my bad dye job into this."

Dean stopped in the hallway, turning slowly and giving her a scathing glare. "Hey, my mom did that to me and that's the last time you get to see anything personal, Missy."

Roni opened her mouth to respond and snapped it shut again as he walked away. Muttering an oath, she took off her glasses and threw them on the table, her frustration evident when she shut off her laptop and closed it harder than necessary. It was worthless without access anyway, so she turned off the light and followed Dean's footpath to the bedroom, already contemplating ways of getting her picture back.

*   *   *   *

Getting out of the truck at the convention center, Dean groaned at the chaos that confronted him, his outward unease making Roni laugh as she playfully punched him in the stomach. "Oh, come on. We're on a break, remember?"

Dean grabbed her hand as she started to walk away, his direct gaze saying everything the tease in his voice didn't. "I'm never on a break when it comes to keeping you safe."

Giving his hand a squeeze, she winked at him, holding up a finger as Stephanie started yelling for her at the rear of the trailer. "I know, I'm ten feet off your ass all day, I swear."

Dean laughed as she walked away, his parting comment making her cheeks flame with heat. "Ditto on that, Donavan."

So lecherous were his thoughts that he jumped with guilt when Carol spoke behind him, the accusing tone of her question grasping his attention. "Why exactly are you so worried about keeping her 'safe,' Dean?"

Dean glared at her as she walked around him to open the tack box on the front of the trailer. "You're getting as sneaky as Mom."

Carol turned to shake a bridle at him, her voice suddenly full of scolding. "Who would like a phone call now and then. I get sick of spending half my conversations hearing about how you've forgotten about her and Dad since they moved to Florida. I swear to God, if she moves back …"

Dean held up a hand in surrender and laughed, his question full of genuine curiosity. "Whoa, damn, what did I do to you?"

Carol stepped closer to him, motioning toward the back of the trailer as she lowered her voice. "She's not in protective custody, is she, Dean?"

Dean casually coiled the rope he took from Carol, his response full of his natural reassurance. "I told you, she's here working as a liaison on a case …"

"You also told me there was nothing between you two."

Her anger was throwing him off, and confusion made him defensive as he looked at her in dumbfounded shock. "Christ, make up your mind, would ya?"

Sighing heavily Carol laid a hand on his arm, her tone turning complacent. "I'm not saying I don't like her, Dean. She's a great girl, but eventually she's going to go home. And when she does, I don't think you're going to be able to shrug it off as easily as you believe. I just think you'd be better off distancing yourself from her, on a personal level."

Dean gave her a good glare, his response making her chuckle as Matthew interrupted to drag her away to the concession stand. "Oh, yeah? Well I think you should stick to milking cows."

✳   ✳   ✳   ✳

Knowing Stephanie as he did, Dean didn't have to look too hard to find Roni. The staging area at the end of the arena was a favorite spot for all the riders, and he found her perched on a section of fence, looking beautifully bewildered at the chaos reigning around her. Leaning against her leg, he reveled in her smile when she looked down at him, her excitement evident in her voice as she grabbed his arm for extra support. "You know, you're going to have to tell me what all this is about, right? Stephanie parked me here, then took off on me." Pointing over at the first group of riders prepping their mounts, he laughed at the bewilderment in Roni's voice. "Like that. Why are they getting their horses all hyped up?"

"It's technically for warming them up. This whole event is about speed." Turning to face the arena he pointed to the triangulated barrels waiting in the fresh-tilled dirt. "Once a rider passes a go mark, they're timed while they run their horses in a cloverleaf pattern around the three barrels. When they clear that last barrel, it's wide open till they cross back over that mark. A winning time will be somewhere in the fourteen- or fifteen-second range. If you knock a barrel over, it's a five-second penalty, which is a lot considering they time to the tenth of a second."

Roni gained a newfound respect for the sport, and she whistled low, her tone disbelieving. "That's a wee bit competitive, isn't it?"

Dean chuckled as he helped her down from the fence to find a safer spot on the bleachers. "Yes, it is. This is also why Steph will run three to four horses. Depending on the spacing, she will be spending most of her downtime switching gear."

They barely had time to sit down before the first rider had entered the arena and Roni's attention was undivided as she watched the rider and horse clear the course with agility and speed that she never would have imagined. As soon as the horse crossed back over the line she looked at Dean with a slow grin, her enthusiasm making him chuckle. "Ohhhh, I'm so going to enjoy this."

*   *   *   *

Dean knew as soon as the water stopped running in the shower that Roni wasn't in the cabin, and even as he rushed to dress he wondered why he was worried. After all, she was sitting in the middle of 3500 acres of Colby country. Hell, he almost wished the bastard would show up.

Leaving the cabin, he made his way along the trail to the fall pond, knowing that the twilight of the sunset had drawn Roni to his natural observation nook atop the boulders surrounding the small waterfall. Clearing the trees, he located her just where he'd expected. She was sitting with his black and silver German shepherd diligently slobbering in her lap. What he hadn't expected though was the hostile greeting he received from his own dog and he stopped in his tracks for the brief second it took for Brody to recognize him, his retort full of laughter as he bent to pet the suddenly complacent pet. "Well, first Griffin throws up on me. Now this. I guess that makes it official. Everyone in my family likes you better than me now."

Roni laughed softly, squinting against the waning sun as he sat down beside her on the flat rock. "You just surprised him, that's all."

The seriousness of his response only made her laugh that much harder. "Oh no, it's true. He told me earlier that everyone had taken a vote; and between Matt's guinea pig, Stephanie's cat, Jason's fish, and Carol's raccoon, I had been ousted by the funny-talking girl with the cute dimples. I can only assume he meant you, so …"

Giving him a good nudge, Roni's smile was broad as she gave him a little of his own. "Well, you know I make a knockout first impression, so I don't know why you brought me up here to steal your thunder to begin with."

Glancing at her to respond, Dean was so struck by her beauty that his retort died on his lips. Be it the natural splendor surrounding them or the relaxation of their day, the ease of her smile and the light in her eyes made him feel like he was seeing Roni for the first time, and his tone turned serious as he reached out to brush a curl from her cheek. "You can steal anything you want if it keeps you smiling like that."

There was no way for Roni to fight the blush that warmed her cheeks, her smile as coy as her reply. "And how would that be exactly?"

Dean returned her previous nudge, sarcasm heavy in his voice. "Like you mean it."

His words turned her thoughtful and she looked away as her tone turned solemn. "Why did you bring me here, Dean? I mean, there have to be a hundred places we could have gone. Why here?"

Dean gave her a curious look, his response cautious at best. "We're here because I know without a shadow of a doubt that we're safe here, why?"

Roni gave him a knowing look, a grin easing her accusation. "I just thought maybe you brought me here knowing I would be cut off from the outside world and wouldn't be able to work …"

Dean held up a hand in defense as he interrupted with a chuckle. "Hey, the lack of technology is only a plus …"

Reacting on a sudden insane thought, his voice hardened as he looked at her inquisitively. "Roni, when was the last time you took a day off from this case?"

Trying to be glib, she grinned sheepishly as she looked away. "Including this one?"

Dean didn't know where the emotions came from, but his irritation with her manifested through passion as he grabbed Roni and surprised her with a searing kiss, the lingering anger in his eyes afterward only increasing her confusion as he grabbed her hand and pressed it to her racing heart. "You feel that? You're still alive and you need to stop feeling guilty for it!"

Positive he'd angered her, Dean moved to rise and was shocked when her hold on him tightened, her emotional response muffled by his shirtfront. "It was my fault, Dean …"

Maybe he'd jolted the confession out of her, but for the first time since Emily's murder Roni voiced her darkest fears, tears streaking her cheeks when she pulled away and answered the question in his eyes. "I said his pattern had already become predictable and boasted that it wouldn't take long to catch him. The day after the quote ran in the post, he killed Emily."

Dean took a steadying breath as he pulled her back into his embrace, his voice full of reassurance as he kissed the top of her head. "It wasn't your fault, and you can't keep punishing yourself for what happened." Brushing a tear from her cheek as he cupped her face, Dean's soft words started her tears anew. "You should honor your sister by living each day the way she remembers you, Roni, because you deserve to be happy, and she wouldn't want anything else for you."

Even as the war between guilt and hope raged inside her, she shook her head in defeat, the sadness of her voice making Dean's heart ache. "I can't, Dean …"

Dean grabbed her chin as she tried to turn away, his gaze direct and his voice firm when he responded. "Yes, you can, because if I know nothing else about you, I do know you're not a quitter. I'm going to be there when you catch this creep, Roni. Then I'm going to take you out to celebrate."

Humbled by the unwavering confidence in his gaze, Roni was unable to voice a reply, her response instead being a soul searching kiss that nearly toppled Dean, it was so unexpected. Recovering within seconds, he was quick to react, his arms tightening around her as he pulled her further into his lap, his pulse quickening when her lips became more demanding. Feeling the tug on the button to his jeans, Dean tore his lips from hers, surprise in his voice as he stilled her hands and looked at her inquisitively. "Roni, here?"

Reveling in his shock, she laughed softly as she shrugged, her words a breathless whisper against his ear before she nipped his lobe. "You're the one that wanted me happy, remember?"

He could have argued that she was displacing her emotions, but his forced response only sent his dog off to ensure their privacy. "Brody, guard."

*   *   *   *

Sitting on the porch of the main house, Roni watched the impromptu football game with a broad smile, impressed not only with Dean's athletic abilities but also with those of his nephew, Matthew, who was obviously headed down Dean's collegiate path. For a lad of fourteen he was nearly as tall as both his uncle and father, but his girth made it easy for him to take either off his feet. It was a deed he had just accomplished with a great bit of gusto, and Roni laughed as he crowed arrogantly over his felled uncle.

"Yes, he learned that from Dean, too."

Roni looked up as Carol joined her on the step, her observation given with an easy smile. "I thought that gloat sounded familiar. He's a wonderful athlete, Carol. He must already be the pride of his team …"

Carol's short laugh was sarcastic as she watched her son's movements, her voice taking on a cynical edge. "I wish. I used to fret over him playing ball. Now he's bored with it and wants to start riding bulls. I'm fighting that one tooth and nail though …"

Roni looked at her disbelievingly, her retort full of sarcasm. "You think?"

Carol's laugh was short and cynical, her tone implying she was grateful for the support. "Thank you. I don't know why I had to have kids that strive to break their necks on a daily basis."

Roni's shoulder dipped from Stephanie's weight as she sat on her other side, the teenager's mocking tone full of good-natured fun. "Oh, blah, blah, blah. I don't strive to break my neck. Riding barrels isn't anything like what Matty wants to do, or thinks he wants to do. You let him ride one time, Mom. First time that bull pops him in the chin, he'll be begging to play football."

Carol leaned forward to glare at Stephanie, her tone incredulous. "You think that a broken collar bone, a dislocated shoulder, and two concussions was a walk in the park? Don't act like you're not on a first name basis with half the ER staff."

Stephanie looked at Roni with an expression of angelic innocence, her off-subject question full of hope. "So, do you think you'll be around in a couple of weeks to see me ride in the finals? It would be great if you and Uncle Dean could come."

Carol chuckled at her daughter's attempt to swing the conversation, her response a gentle reminder that Roni was there on borrowed time. "She's not here on vacation, Stephanie. She and Dean have a case to work on, you know."

Stephanie jumped up to answer a ringing phone, her parting remark full of confidence. "Yeah, but it won't take them long to crack that puppy."

Carol was quick to notice the flicker of something in Roni's eyes before the shield went up, and for the first time she couldn't help but wonder the nature of the case that had brought her to their doorstep. It wasn't long before her natural curiosity prompted her soft question. "How long have you been on this case, Roni?"

Taking a steadying breath Roni kept her eyes averted, her gaze locked on the game she did not see as she responded truthfully. "Some days it feels like forever, like a nightmare that I can never seem to wake from."

Carol squeezed her shoulder, genuine concern in her reply. "I hope it ends soon for you then."

Sighing heavily, Roni gave herself a mental shake and looked at Carol with a forced smile, trying her best to regain some of her previous mirth as she changed the subject. "Me too, I have to say it helped coming here. I've had such a wonderful time that I don't want to leave, and I can't thank you enough for your hospitality, Carol."

Both of them jumped when a waywardly tipped football barely missed Roni's head and bounced off the porch rail. Carol's response was full of amusement as Matthew ran up to get it. "Well, you're welcome here anytime. We've enjoyed your company, despite what Matty says."

Matthew chuckled, grinning down at Roni as he spun the football on his index finger, boyish charm playing in his brown eyes as he revisited his taunting. "Hey, I can always use another girl around for target practice."

Dean unceremoniously hit Matt with a cross block that sent the boy stumbling. His voice was full of laughter as he sat on the step behind Roni. "Watch it before you get used for practice yourself, dough head." As he tugged on Roni's ponytail, her brow arched in question as she looked up at him. "So, are you about ready to head back to the evil city?"

Roni gave him a good-natured glare, sighing dramatically as she responded. "Jeez, work, work, work. Can't you let me relax every now and then?"

Her statement launched Dean into a fit of laughter that no one else quite understood, but he didn't care. He chose rather to leave the moment private and his family pondering his strange behavior.

✳   ✳   ✳   ✳

Slinging a bag into the back of the truck, Dean closed the hatch and turned to find Roni standing on the cobbled walk of the cabin, a wistful look on her face as she glanced around one more time. Somehow he'd known that underneath that lab coat was a girl that would have a deep appreciation for nature, and he was once again glad he'd brought her here.

Roni turned for the truck and grinned at the look on his face, her voice chiding as he opened her door. "So you're just going to grin at me like the Cheshire cat? No 'I told you so'?"

Dean shrugged slightly, his grin spreading as he took her backpack and helped her in. "Nah, not my style. I'm just glad you had a good time."

Roni put a hand over his as he moved to close the door, her voice growing soft. "I really did, Dean. Thank you so much for sharing your family with me. They're such wonderful people."

Dean nodded in agreement, leaning into the truck to kiss her soundly before replying. "Yes, they are, and you're very welcome." Walking around the truck, he got in and started it up, turning to look at her with a solemn expression. "You know it helps me, being surrounded by so much death, to come out here every now and then and be reminded of what life is about."

It was the look in Dean's eyes that impacted her most, and above everything else she finally knew the real reason he'd brought her here. Giving him a crooked smile, she nodded slightly, a lilt of sarcasm in her retort. "Yeah, I hear ya, Cowboy. Point taken."

CHAPTER 7

▼

Secure behind the mirrored tint of the building, he watched Colby get out of the truck and scan his surroundings, and he could tell it wasn't a conscious action. Natural alertness couldn't be taught. It was bred into predators, like himself. Opening the door, he helped Veronica out, all the while keeping an observant eye on their environment. At least he was good. Although she was talking nonstop, he never diverted his attention from his objective, steering her toward the nearest entrance to the building. Her animated hand movements and facial expressions brought a smile to his face. He'd missed watching her, seeing the way a good puzzle lit her eyes with life. His smile froze, the shift of Colby's hand suddenly catching his attention. The possessive way his fingers curled around her waist almost made him groan out loud. Damn, complications. He hated complications.

Dean pushed the elevator button, glancing at his watch as he looked around again. Something was giving him the creeps—something or someone. The doors opened and he followed Roni inside, his tone casual as he tried to shake the feeling. "I didn't see Lyn's car, did you?"

Roni gave him a horrified look, her thoughts instantly reverting to the discussion about the picture. "You didn't really bring that hideous picture, did you? I knew I should have destroyed that thing."

Dean patted his chest pocket, his smile broad and his tone cocky. "You'd have never found it, Sunshine."

Glancing up at the floor indicator, Roni grabbed Dean by his tie, yanked him down, and waylaid him with a searing kiss. When she was sure he was good and dazed, she abruptly released him, smiled, and just as she'd timed it, turned and made her exit as the doors slid open.

Dean caught up with her seconds later, his expression anything but schooled. "What the hell was that?"

Roni looked up at him with her sweetest smile, her answer unenlightening. "Let's just say it was a lesson learned."

Dean was starting to get nervous. "A lesson learned?"

Roni noticed Mason step from his office, his arm rising when he saw them, and she nodded at Dean in response. "Yup, now smile because Mason's motioning for us."

Dean gritted his teeth and nearly growled as she walked away. She had to be the most frustrating woman he'd ever met, and he didn't have a clue as to what to do with her. Taking a breath he followed, looking at Mason questioningly when Roni veered into his office and shut the door behind her. Mason answered with a solemn nod, resignation in his tone. "I think all hell's about to bust loose."

Opening his mouth to ask what he meant, Dean snapped it shut when the shouting began and he actually took a step backwards at the tone of the man inside. "Who the hell's in there?"

The man in question walked in front of the window, and Dean knew exactly who he was, and he was fighting the insane urge to run when Mason responded. "Finneas Rourke has come to take his daughter home. I guess we'll see how that goes."

*   *   *   *

Roni faced her father toe to toe, her temper the only one in the house that came near to matching his. "What in the hell are you doing here?"

Finn struggled with his anger, his tone authoritative as he faced his daughter's apparent anger. "No matter what, remember I'm still your father, Veronica. I've come to take you home."

Roni shook her head, her short laugh cynical. "Like hell you are. You didn't get this information from a passport trace, Da. How the hell did you find out?"

Finn's interest piqued at her slip and he played her for information. "I have my ways, you know that. Are you okay?"

She tossed her dark hair, her chin raising a notch in stubbornness. "I'm fine. You know damn well a few words won't scare me away. I don't ..."

Her mouth snapped shut when his fist fell to his palm and his temper erupted. "Dammit, Veronica, is he already contacting you? I told you to keep a low profile. What in God's name have you been doing, holding bloody press conferences?"

Roni shouted back just as loudly, her aggravation apparent in her tone. "No, did you fly all the way here to criticize the way I do my job?" Taking a breath Roni reigned in her anger, her voice softening when she continued. "I went to one crime scene in the middle of the night, and if you didn't know about the message, then what are you doing here?"

She watched the play of emotions cross his still handsome features and was uncomfortable at his reluctance to talk, his question a mere distraction to gather his thoughts. "Do you want to sit down?"

Roni held up her hands in frustration, a newfound edge in her voice. "No, I want you to tell me what you're doing here before you make me a nervous wreck. Is everyone okay at home?"

It was then that he saw the concern in her eyes and he was quick to assure her. "Yes, everyone's fine. Well, your mother's upset with me right now, but she'll be okay once you're … you're home."

His nervousness amused her and Roni was sure she was witnessing a first, Finneas Rourke stammering. "And what's got her upset Da?"

Finneas took a deep breath and looked his daughter in the eye, his resolve unwavering. "Roni, I want you to come home. Get off this case, right now. Is there any chance you will cooperate with me?"

She shook her head, her eyes sparkling with curiosity. "Nah, no chance, especially now."

Glancing out the window at the two agents standing guard and shooting the breeze, he smiled knowingly. "You care to elaborate? I was watching from upstairs when you two arrived …"

Not falling for the bait, Roni's eyes squinted suspiciously, her voice softening as she held her course. "No, I don't care to elaborate. Now, why is Mum upset?"

He sighed heavily, his response sending her thoughts careening in every direction. "Because she found out you're in Denver. I was holding out hope that you being here was purely coincidental, but that's been shot to hell now."

Roni felt a numbness growing in the pit of her stomach, and her response had a hollow ring to it. "How? And why would she be upset because I'm here?"

When he tried to turn away from her, Roni grabbed his hand, her grip firm as she forced her father to look at her. "What's going on?"

Shaking his head with concern, Finneas reached into his pocket and pulled out the envelope that had sent his life into a tailspin, handing it to her with a heavy sigh. "I'm sorry, sweetheart. I was assured that the hospital records were sealed, and I was never supposed to have this conversation with you."

Roni took the envelope that was strangely enough addressed to her mother and opened it with a shaking hand. Unsure of what to expect, evidence of finger-print testing and her father's comment had her handling the scrap of newsprint as if it were toxic. And it was. Not only was she reading a birth announcement for herself from an American newspaper, the red-inked dates printed across it insinu-ated her impending death, and her blood ran cold to know her mother had seen it.

It was Finn's turn to stop her when she stepped away, the look on her face making his confession that much harder. "I was here on assignment and landed in the hospital, Veronica. Your mother traveled against doctor's advice and ended up going into premature labor." He grasped her arms when she tried to jerk away, continuing with an apologetic note in his voice. "I was so incensed that you were born here that when we got back to Ireland I had the records changed to show you being born the day we returned. I'm so sorry, honey. Like I said, this was something I never expected to resurface, and I thought it was a non-issue."

Roni felt like her head had just exploded. The killer's message had suddenly taken on a whole new meaning, and this meant every drop of blood somehow had something to do with her. She literally felt sick to her stomach. "Why were you here? What happened to you?"

Finn grimaced, shaking his head no. "I can't tell you. I signed confid …"

Cutting him off, her eyes turned into blue ice as she jerked her arm free of his grasp. "Never mind, I should have known better than to ask. My whole life has been classified in some way or another, and now you want to tell me it's all been a lie too?"

Finn's voice turned commanding as he blocked her departure. "Now wait a minute …"

Roni froze, her soft voice hard as she glared at him. "No, I won't wait. Do you know every American victim was born at Castle Rock Memorial? Do you know that he left me a message scrawled on a dead girl that read, 'I knew you'd come *home* to me'? Do you know that this means that every girl murdered here has been an effort to get me to follow him here? And for what, for this?"

She finished by shaking the crumpled paper at him, and Finn ran a hand through his graying hair, his usual confidence taking a hit under her direct gaze. "I don't know, Veronica. I don't have any answers yet, sweetheart …"

Roni choked back the sob that rose in her throat, her response bitter. "I had answers and you wouldn't listen. Now it's too late."

Muttering an oath, his reply was immediately defensive. "There was no motive, no connection to your case …"

Turning for the door, Roni's voice was full of anger. "The game is his motive. Go home. I don't need your help, and I'm sure the hell not going anywhere before I find out who's doing this. I'll call Mum and settle her down, but you should have saved yourself the trip."

Sidestepping his attempts to stop her, she stalked past Mason and Dean, ignored her father's angry command for her to come back, and headed for the elevator without a backward glance.

She was so lost in her livid thoughts, it took a full thirty seconds before she realized Dean was standing beside her on the elevator, and he smiled at her surprised look. "Where are we goin'?"

Roni's voice was a bare whisper as she struggled to control her emotions. "I'm going home to do some research."

Dean scratched his head and gave her an animated expression, his voice slightly teasing. "Isn't that what we do *here*? Research, investigation …?"

Roni looked up at him and was surprised when tears blurred her vision, her retort forced through a throat clogged with emotion. "I just can't be here right now."

Regardless of cameras or departmental policies, Dean reached out and took her hand, his fingers entwining hers before he raised it to his lips and kissed it, his soft question actually making Roni laugh. "Well, can I have my wallet back so I can drive you home then?"

*   *   *   *

When they hit the apartment door Roni went straight to the kitchen, and Dean sighed heavily when he heard ice hit the glass. Locking the door behind him he threw the keys on the bar, taking his jacket off as he walked to the kitchen. "What's wrong?"

Roni poured a good bit of scotch in a glass, her response void of emotion when she looked up at him. "I need to call my mother. Can I use your mobile?"

Dean nodded as he turned it over, asking, "Is everything all right?"

The honest concern in his voice was the only reason she answered his question. Roni opened her mouth to speak and found her words blocked by emotion, her reply merely a strangled noise as she walked away. "No."

Roni returned a good bit later, looking red-eyed and still not willing to talk. She sat at the table and began working with her computer, her half empty glass on one side and a cigarette burning on the other. Dean shook his head with confusion. She cut him off with a glassy glare, and he knew that her harsh retort was nothing more than a defensive tactic. "You should go back to work. The boys are outside, and I'll be fine."

Dean snorted at her as he sat at the table, disbelief heavy in his voice as he held up his hands and gave her a shrug. "Whatever. I'm working here too, Roni. It's just up to you whether or not I help. I can go take a nap while you drink yourself silly, or you can tell me what's going on and we work this out together."

Roni covered her face as her eyes welled with tears, a near sob distorting her response. "I feel like the rug's just been pulled out from under me, Dean. I'm losing control and I don't know what's going on anymore."

Dean reached over and rubbed the top of her head, his voice dropping as his heart softened. "Sweetheart, I hate to break it to you, but you've never been in control here. He has. And until you accept that—that this is his game and that he's using you as his pawn—you'll never be able to win."

Roni sighed heavily and gave him a knowing look, then made her soft confession. "I was born at Castle Rock Memorial."

Dean sat back with a thud as he took the scrap of paper she handed him, the words in front of him dropping his jaw. Roni gave him a weak laugh and nodded in agreement to his reaction. "Yeah, nice touch, huh? So, not only has my father lied to me my entire life, it's a serial killer that gets to spring it on me. And that also explains why he sends me roses."

The last she said more to herself as an observation, her attention returning to the computer with a renewed vengeance. Dean stared at her blankly for a few seconds before he realized she wasn't going to continue and reached over to pick up her cigarette, taking a much-needed drag as his sympathy for her increased tenfold. "Wow, so can I get you another drink?"

Roni glanced up from her computer with a slight grin, her resilient attitude impressing Dean that much more. "Nah, I think my flash of self pity has passed. Now I just want to find out who's doing this, and why."

Dean nodded in agreement, loosening his tie as he eyed the announcement with speculation. "Yes, especially now that he's threatened your life, again."

Roni glanced up at him with a heavy sigh, her thoughts drifting to the recipient of said threat. "He sent it to my mum, Dean. The poor woman is beside herself."

Dean nodded absently, his thoughts turning curious. "I can only imagine. So, what were Mom and Pop doing in Colorado, anyway?"

Roni rolled her eyes dramatically, her voice dripping with sarcasm. "What I've been told is that Da was here on assignment and somehow ended up in the hospital. My mother flew against doctor's orders and ended up going into premature labor."

Dean chewed on his lip for a second before responding, curiosity heavy in his voice. "It's possible, Roni. NORAD is very close to Castle Rock. You think he got injured on the job? It had to have been pretty serious for your mom to put you or herself in jeopardy."

Roni gave him a thoughtful look as she shrugged, a note of bitterness still in her voice when she responded. "I don't know, maybe. I asked him what he was doing here and he told me it was classified. He had their hospital records sealed and a new birth certificate made for me when we arrived home from the States in early June. Obviously he never expected anyone to have reason to inquire about it. Are you going to give my smoke back?"

Dean took another drag before handing it back, exhaling smoke rings before replying. "God, I miss smoking. I can run faster, but I still miss it. So where do we start? I say with the picture. Somewhere in your college years is a man you rejected, scorned, made fun of, something that set you apart from the other dye bottle blondes."

Roni gave him a dubious glare, her tone full of hurt. "Hey, watch it, don't make me call Carol for your picture." With a sudden idea she snapped her fingers, reaching for his cell phone she had laid on the table. "Can I use this again?" Dean's hand fell on hers as he laughed sarcastically and Roni scoffed at his immediate thought. "I need to call London, not your sister."

He knew without asking she wanted privacy from big brother and released her hand with a curious nod. Roni's fingers dialed the number automatically, her eyes scanning the University's website, hoping something or someone would strike a chord. Seth's sleepy voice answered on the fifth ring, and Roni smiled despite herself. "I can always depend on you to be loafing around the flat, can't I, love?"

Seth's wit was forever sharp, his reply dulled only by sleep. "Except when I'm fetching mail and feeding the neighbor's bloody fish. Oh, bullocks, this is my neighbor, isn't it?"

Roni couldn't help but laugh. "Seth, you know Brutus and I love you. I promise to bring you a tee shirt, okay? Now, I need a really important favor. Do you have the time?"

Seth chuckled in response, extreme amusement in his voice when he replied. "What exactly would I be doing? You know I'm a completely worthless bloke."

Thinking about his revolutionary paintings, Roni was quick to reassure him. "You're not worthless, Seth. Someday you'll be famous and until then, Brutus and I would be lost without you. Go to my flat and look in my closet. There's a box labeled 'Yearbooks' on the top right shelf. I need you to ship them to me overnight. I really need these, so don't forget. There should be a few hundred quid in the cookie tin. You ready to write down the address?"

She heard him shuffling around and could almost see him moving about in his cluttered studio apartment, half-painted canvases littering the walls and floors. "Relax, love, I think I can handle shipping a couple of books."

Roni gave him the address, chatted for a few more minutes, then signed off, promising to return with paint and brushes for him, and gourmet fish food for her neglected goldfish.

Handing the phone back to Dean, he was glad to see her color starting to look a little more normal when she looked at him with a small smile. "Well, that will help with the college years anyway. I need to go back over those crime scene pictures again too, to make sure I'm not missing anyone that looks familiar."

Dean started to respond and stopped when his phone rang, his tone curt when he answered. "Colby"

"Dean, its Lyn. Is Roni okay?" Dean chuckled as she continued without giving him the chance to respond. "Of course she isn't, don't answer that. Her father's gone but he left us with a shitload of files that are going to turn the tide of this investigation. You don't know how badly I need her here right now."

Dean sighed heavily, his hand raking through his short dark hair. "Yes, I do, but I'm not pushing it. Any luck on identifying the new victim?"

Lyn sighed with aggravation, a near pout in her voice. "Yeah, here. Ty wants to talk to you."

Tyler's voice came over the line and Dean could hear the pride he felt over his accomplishments. "Deano, tell Roni we've identified the latest victim, and she was born at the same hospital. I've already started culling out all females born there 15 to 17 years ago, give me an email address and I'll send this program over."

Dean looked at Roni as he chewed on his lip, telling Tyler to hold for a second. "Ty wants to send you the file on last vic. Do you want it?"

Dean nodded speculatively to her laptop and Roni shook her head, her anger renewing a little. "No, I want to check my hard drive first. Was she a match?"

With Dean's nod, she frowned, glancing at her watch. "Tell him to start a list of girls born at least 16 years ago at Castle Rock, and let's try to get up to speed with this guy."

Dean chuckled, amused at how in sync she already was with their team. "He already has."

Mirroring his grin, her brow rose in speculation. "Well then, tell him we'll be back in a few hours to start going over them. That should give me enough time to find out how my father is gaining inside information."

Dean relayed that to Tyler and hung up, watching in amazement as Roni changed before his eyes. With a twist of her hair and her glasses in place, the pity party was over and she went to work. Her first step was to scour her files for any ghostwriter programs her father may have loaded onto her laptop. An hour later he was chuckling as she started taking the thing apart, spreading parts on the tabletop. "Are you sure you know what you're doing? We can call the store and go buy you a new one if it would be easier."

She gave him an evil look over the rim of her glasses, her grin full of self-confidence. "I carry a backup C-drive with me, so it won't take that long to switch it out if I have to. You'd be amazed at what I can do, Colby."

Dean leaned backward in his chair, shaking his head as he smirked at her. "Nah, not really, but you, however, would be amazed at the things I know about you."

Her screwdriver froze and she looked up at him, her eyes suspicious. "Oh yeah? What do you think you know about me?"

Dean smiled as he linked his fingers behind his head, his voice low and self-confident. "I know you're hardheaded, brilliant, loyal, beautiful, speak at least four languages ..."

Roni interrupted in a disbelieving tone, her eyes growing wary. "How do you know that?"

Dean gave her a knowing wink, his response easing her suspicions. "Because I also know you talk in your sleep, but not in English—everything but. From what I can understand, there's Russian, German, French, and some other language I've never heard, ever. I think you made that one up ..."

Roni suppressed her laughter long enough to ask him a question in her native tongue. "Is ea b'fheidir Gaeilge?"

Dean nodded as he pointed a finger at her. "Yep, that's the one. What is that? You spend half the night talking in that one. The others come in spurts. It's like sleeping in a foreign film festival, without the subtitles."

Roni shook her head as she tried to control her laughter, wiping away the tears that spilled from the corner of her eyes. "It's Gaelic, my grandmother's language."

Dean shook his head in amazement, his response laced with awe. "Well you must dream about her a lot. I don't know how you do it. I can barely speak English and Spanish, much less keep up with four."

Roni dismissed her talent for academics with a light shrug, her nerves beginning to settle a little with their light conversation. "I have this thing about retaining information; I never forget anything."

Dean laughed as he leaned back in his chair, his grateful tone full of implication. "Well that's a good thing to know. Any other tricks I should know about?"

Roni looked up at him coyly through her lashes, her impish grin making his heart lurch. "You already know I'm a pretty good pickpocket, but I'm also pretty good with locks, and I could hotwire a car if I had to."

Dean ran a hand over his face as he chuckled. "Why the hell would you need to hotwire a car? And who taught you these illegal tricks anyway?"

Roni nearly cheered when she found the keystroke logger hidden in her hardware, her brilliant smile throwing him off as she answered. "They're only illegal if you use them to commit a crime." Removing the tiny piece of spyware, she held it up for Dean to see, a touch of sarcasm edging her voice. "See, anywhere else this would be illegal, but my father thinks that it's protection."

Dean reached out and accepted the device, his tone absent-minded as he examined it. "He's gone, by the way. Lyn said he left a shitload of files that she wants your help with, whenever you're ready."

Roni paused in shock then began to reassemble her laptop with vigor, responding in a tone full of conviction. "I'm ready now because I'm not going to give him what he wants, Dean. We have too much to do for me to freak out right now. I've had two days off and I'm going to go in there and look at this with a fresh mind and a new attitude, because that bloody bastard has finally made a mistake."

Dean couldn't help but chuckle at her fighting spirit and prodded her on with a verbal nudge. "And what, pray tell, would that be?"

The fire in her eyes was back as she closed her laptop with a satisfied grin, her reply confident. "He made my father believe me."

CHAPTER 8

▼

When Roni and Dean entered the control room she lost a step when she saw Emily's medical report displayed across the giant screen in the room and her startled look made Lyn feel guilty for going through it without waiting; but then, she'd had no idea when to expect them either. Giving Roni a chance to compose herself, Dean quickly handed Tyler the picture from his wallet, asked him to scan it, and launched into their findings as she took a seat. He was mentally kicking himself for not calling Mason to let him know they were on the way, and from the look his boss was giving him, he felt the same way. "This picture was taken of Roni and her sister while she was attending Oxford University. It could be nothing. But along with the information we received this morning, it could be everything."

Dean looked at Roni as he took his seat beside her, the encouragement in his gaze willing her to continue. Taking a calming breath she did so tentatively. "You all know my father was here this morning, but not the purpose of his visit. He was here to tell me that I too was born at Castle Rock Memorial, and to take me home. Needless to say he's leaving with only one of his missions accomplished." Taking a deep breath she looked around at the shocked faces and gave them a few moments to recover before she continued. "And so, with these new revelations we can all assume that my being here is not by mistake but by design. Dean also believes the trigger could have happened during the short time I sported blonde hair in college, so we can start there, I guess."

Lyn looked at the picture on the wall with newfound interest, her sharp eyes full of enlightenment when she looked at Roni. "Now I understand the inconsistencies of your sister's case. If this is someone that is fixated on you, he's probably

been watching you for years. You said you were at your parents that night for dinner. Maybe Emily stumbled upon him, coming home from the game that night.
She was dropped off in front of the house. Maybe he was there. She stumbled
upon him and he had to kill her. That would explain the lack of stab wounds and
the evident remorse he showed by leaving her body in the churchyard. The over-
abundance of flowers could have been his apology to you for her death."

Roni swallowed the lump in her throat, her eyes hard as she shook her head.
"His apology is not accepted." Clearing her throat she flipped through the pages
of her notepad, finding the list she'd been working on. "I was involved with
numerous activities that particular semester, but the Varsity Games commanded
the majority of my free time since I represented several different societies."

Quietly studying the information splayed across the wall, Mason, as a father
himself, felt pity for the man he'd met that day. Hell, he was half tempted to put
Roni on a plane himself, and his thoughts made his voice gruffer when he spoke.
"Then let's concentrate on the games. I want a list of every person you competed
against, in every category, and by what margins. This could be retribution or
admiration. Donavan, I want to see you in my office before you get started."

Mason stood and gathered his things, his actions signaling the end of the
meeting and the cue for the team to go to work. As Roni rose to follow him she
caught Dean's reassuring wink and smiled despite herself, her step a bit lighter as
she walked out.

*   *   *   *

Closing Mason's door behind her, Roni decided to get a jump on him with an
apology for the drama she had brought into his office. "I want to apologize for
walking out this morning. I honestly didn't know how to handle the situation."

Mason took a deep breath, his eyes full of understanding when he looked at
her. "Donavan, I know this is a blow to you, but try to take it easy on your father.
He's already lost one daughter and knows for sure the killer is fixated on you
now. Maybe he didn't quite know how to handle the situation either. Do you
think it was easy for him to leave here, knowing what could happen to you? It
took me a long time to convince him you were in capable hands. But bottom
line, he left because he knows if you are ever to forgive him, he has to let you see
this through." Taking an envelope from his drawer he handed it to her, his tone
slightly chiding as he nodded toward it. "Obviously he knew he wouldn't get to
speak his peace though, because he left this for you." Pausing for a instant, he
leaned against his desk, his arms crossing over his chest as his expression turned

even more serious. "Now for the other issue. Your father gave us copies of the files, Veronica; and still, it seems you've been holding back."

The look that passed over her face was almost painful, her insulted retort cutting him off. "I gave you everything I could get, which wasn't that easy with the restric ..."

Realizing too late she was digging her own grave, she clammed up, leaving Mason nodding solemnly. "That's what I figured, but not what I'm talking about." Picking up a folder on his desk, he handed it to her, his tone hardening with accusation as she glanced through copies of the all too familiar letters. "Let's talk about these, Donavan. This pattern does not constitute a few letters and threats. I pulled this file because I need all of my agents focused right now. But you know if you'd shared this with us to begin with, we'd have known this guy is obsessed with you and we'd be one step closer to catching his sorry ass."

Roni nodded, studying the toe of her shoe for a second before she gathered her courage and apologized. "I'm sorry, Mason. I just didn't want to sensationalize my involvement with the case any more than necessary. It was bad enough that Em was my sister, but I swear that I had no idea I was at the root of this."

Mason cut her short, reading the guilt in her voice and scoffing at it. "Donavan, you may as well apologize for the rain. We're dealing with an unstable person here, and you can't control what drives him. What I need is for you to go out there and be open-minded, and work closely with Lyn now. With you for guidance, she can pinpoint her profile and narrow our target. We're getting close, real close."

Roni smiled as she nodded in agreement, appreciating the pep talk she now realized she was there for. "I have my Oxford yearbooks en route from London, as well as a few new search programs I'm working on. I'm hoping we can find a lead there."

Mason pushed from the desk to see her to the door, his voice reassuring. "Good, the yearbooks should be a good source. Maybe something will jog your memory if you're looking at pictures." Putting his hand on the doorknob, he paused, his expression again all business when he looked at her. "And one other thing, you go nowhere but here and home—nowhere. No gyms, no restaurants, no ice cream parlors. I've given my word and I'm not giving this man a chance, do you understand?"

Roni smiled despite the anger bursting in her gut. She respected him too much to argue with his orders, but her retort still had a cynical ring to it. "You sure you don't want to put an ankle band on me while you're at it?"

Mason gave her a smile and a wink as he opened the office door, never missing a beat. "I'm working on it."

Roni laughed him off and made a hasty retreat, silently praying he was only kidding.

*   *   *   *

Walking into the control room, Roni shook her head in dismay to see her graduation picture on the big screen. "Now this is embarrassing. I expect to see school pictures from each and every one of you to make up for it."

Dean looked up from the computer printout Ty had handed him, his grin broad. "Three-year fencing champion, karate, kendo, pistols ... I thought the Varsity Games were field hockey, soccer, cricket ..."

"The Games are about many things, but mainly about skill, tact, and teamwork," Roni said, grinning as she took her seat, shaking her head slowly. "The school paper also ran the Sleuth games at the same time. They were my favorites and what I concentrated the most energy on."

Tyler looked up from his computer screen, his brows furrowed. "Yeah, I'm not coming up with anything in the school register on that."

Roni colored slightly, revealing her somewhat geekier side. "It was a role playing game hosted by the students. Two groups team up. One masterminds the evil deed, and the other solves it. You know, a Holmes and Watson thing."

Dean grinned as he nudged her foot under the table. "Role playing, huh?"

Coloring slightly Roni threw him an incensed glare, thankful that Lyn seemed unaware of Dean's taunt, and pressed on. "So there could be someone still playing?" Lyn asked. "Are there any records of the people who participated?"

Roni shook her head, trying to bring her past back to life, a spark lighting her eyes as she pointed to Tyler. "Back issues of the paper. Go to the website; they have a link."

Ty nodded, his fingers already clicking away. "I'm on it. This is going to take a while if you guys have something else to do."

Roni, for one, wanted to go down to the lab to see if Juni had been able to lift any prints off the last victim, and she stood to gather her notes. "Yeah, I'd like to run to the lab and check in with Juni, if we have a bit."

Dean motioned for her to wait as he scooted his chair back. "I'm going to the range. I'll go down with you."

Roni nodded and turned to Lyn with a questioning gaze, trying to keep her tone neutral as she forced herself onto the proverbial couch. "Would you have a couple hours later?"

Lyn was thrilled that Roni had taken the first step and her smile was broad as she nodded enthusiastically. "Oh sure, anytime you're ready, just come on by."

Passing Ty a couple notes on shortcuts to the O.U. website, Roni gave him a wink and followed Dean out of the room. Getting on the elevator, she was lost in her thoughts and totally unprepared for Dean's anger when the doors closed. "Why the hell aren't you carrying a gun? You have the training, the obvious skill from your marks, and you have a stalker. *Why* aren't you armed?"

Roni shook her head slightly, her eyes round with surprise. "I, uh ... I don't ... well, because you have a gun. Besides, I'm not that kind of agent."

His gruff response was clear indication that he wasn't satisfied with her answer. "Why aren't you?"

Exhaling heavily she turned to him with an exasperated tone. "You need to make up your mind. Either I can be a super agent, or I can stay out of danger. I can't do both, so I'll be a doctor and nail their asses with forensic science. And yes, just in case you were wondering, you did, you sounded just like my father."

Dean shook his head and tried to clear out the mess he was making of the situation. "I'm sorry. I guess I have trouble with all of this skill going to waste. You would be a great intelligence agent."

Roni gave him a glare, her tone icy. "I don't consider the rapists and murderers I've helped put away a waste of my skills."

Dean ran a hand through his hair in exasperation. "You know I didn't mean ..."

The doors opened and with another glare, she was gone, leaving him in mid sentence. He was starting to get used to it. With a heavy sigh and a low groan he followed her path to the lab, almost running into her as he opened the door. Coming up short he noticed two things at once, the shallow basket of roses on Juni's desk and the stricken look on Roni's face.

Juni walked in from the other examination room, her smile wide as she nudged Dean in the side. "Way to go, Romeo."

Dean's brows furrowed as he shook his head and headed for the flowers. "They're not from me."

Juni felt the color drain from her face as she looked at Roni, suddenly noticing that she too was as white as a sheet. "Jesus, Roni, sit down."

Juni's voice drew Roni back to reality, and with a shake of her head she walked over to the desk on shaky legs. "I'm okay. When did they come? Who brought them?"

Juni shrugged, answering with a voice that was now a little unsteady. "I came in from the back a couple hours earlier and they were here. I assumed …"

She motioned to Dean as he followed Roni's lead, his eyes locking with hers as they gingerly unfolded the tissue around the leafless stems of the blood red roses. "There's no card."

Her voice was low, her eyes pooling with tears as she shook her head in defeat. "No, this is it."

Dean instinctively drew her to him, his reassuring embrace making her feel better. "I will never, ever send you roses."

Roni half grinned, wiping the tear that slipped away with the back of her hand. "Make sure you don't."

Giving him a little wink she cleared her throat and looked at Juni's still stricken expression. "He probably paid some kid to deliver them. I want to dust them and run them under the ultraviolet light. I'm hoping for a mistake soon. He has to have touched one of these thorns, cutting off all the leaves."

Dean was anxious to view the department's surveillance tapes from the morning, so he decided to skip practice for the security office, his excuse absently given as he turned to leave. "I'm going to view some surveillance and ask some questions. Page me if you need me."

Juni and Roni both nodded, their attention already drawn to preparing the equipment for their project. They were the same in that aspect: when they wanted to accomplish something, they had tunnel vision.

*   *   *   *

Dean found Roni hours later in Lyn's office, his light tap on the door only meant to draw their attention as he stepped inside. "You guys going to work all night?"

Lyn checked her watch and was surprised by the time, jumping up to gather her things. "Shit, I had no idea that it was that late. I hate running out on you but I promised my kid I'd be home for dinner tonight."

Roni waved her off, stifling a yawn herself. "Don't be silly. We can start fresh tomorrow when the books arrive. I know there was a whole section on the Games."

Lyn nodded absently, her tone confident as she slid on her coat. "Good. Maybe by this time tomorrow evening, we'll have a name for our busy little gardener."

Roni stood and started gathering her files, not surprised when Lyn said good night and left them standing in her office. She'd never met such open and trusting people. They were more than colleagues, they were almost like a small family and the atmosphere appealed to her. "Did you find out anything?"

Dean shook his head as he squatted down to dig her shoe out from under the couch, a touch of annoyance in his voice. "No, you were right. The tapes showed some kid, maybe fourteen. When the receptionist insisted on a florist's name, he said, "You Pick." She wrote down 'You Pick Flowers.' I think she misunderstood his intent."

Roni chuckled, grabbing his arm for support as she slid on her pump. "Yeah, I'd think. There were prints on the basket handle. Of course they were juvenile prints, but I'm scanning them anyway. If we can find him, he may be able to describe our killer."

Dean gave her a look, his tone sarcastic. "I've had the DPD looking at his picture for about three hours now. What do you want to eat? We'll have to pick something up on the way home."

Roni leaned over to turn off the lamp on the side table, throwing him a sidelong look. "I see Mr. Martin had a talk with you too?"

He chuckled as he ushered her out of Lyn's office, closing the door behind them. "You know he did, and he was none too happy about the flowers. He's sure this loon has lured you here just to kill you." Her footsteps slowed and he stopped, his sharp eyes concentrating on her expression. "What do you think about that?"

Roni fought the panic that rose in her chest and swallowed the lump in her throat. It had been her first thought when her father told her where she was born. They all felt the same and it was time to stop dancing around the truth. "I think we better find him before he's ready to end the game."

Dean put a hand on her lower back and steered toward the elevator, his tone calm and comforting, his breath warm against her ear. "You don't think for one minute I'm going to let anything happen to you, do you?"

Roni waited for the elevator doors to close before she looked up at him with a mischievous grin, her thoughts remaining a mystery. "I think I'd like some Chinese food tonight. That place you like on 28th has great soup. I'd love something hot and spicy."

Dean's brow shot up and he shook his head, his voice full of humor. "No problem there, kiddo. Just let me get some food in me first."

Giving him a sidelong look, her smile broadened. "I was talking about the food."

Dean escorted her from the elevator, his eyes constantly scanning the parking garage as he continued to the truck. "Really? I thought for sure you were talking about something else."

Roni grinned at him as she got in the truck, the look in her eyes just as smoldering as his, even if her voice didn't reflect it. "Oh yeah, well, you know, that's what you get for thinking."

Dean shook his head as she shut her door, his chuckle echoing in the half empty structure. "Nice, Donavan, real nice."

*   *   *   *

Roni twisted the key in the lock as she juggled the food and mail in her hands. Opening the door she took one step, froze, and stepped backwards, her brow furrowing at the manila envelope lying on the floor with her footprint in the middle of it.

Dean nudged her forward, his tone playfully grumpy. "Move it, lady. I'm hungry."

Roni retrieved the envelope, stepping aside so he could enter. "Sorry, we had a delivery."

Dean set the sack down and turned as she closed and locked the door behind her. He noticed immediately she held the envelope by the slightest bit of corner. "You think it's from him?"

Roni shrugged, her smile forced as she crossed to the kitchen for better light. "It could be a complaint from the neighbors about the noise last night, but you can never be too sure."

Dean handed her a pair of gloves from her briefcase and watched with an anxious expression. "Personally, I hope it's from the neighbors."

Roni grinned despite herself, the seriousness of his tone tickling her. Her smile faded when she pulled a negative proof sheet from the envelope, her breath catching as she saw the word "Whore" scrawled across the sheet in red magic marker. Holding it up to the light, her look of disgust turned to horror as she looked up at Dean. "He's been watching us, and I mean *watching* us, Dean."

Dean snatched her hands closer to the light, his jaw dropping to see the pictures of him and Roni together. There were pictures of them getting in and out of the car, pictures of them at the gym and eating in restaurants, and even a couple of them that were very compromising. He remembered that night vividly—the rain, the candles, the open blinds. He nearly choked on the revulsion that welled within him, sighing heavily as he reached for the phone. "I'll have an agent check out the apartment building across the street. That's the only place he could have gotten those shots."

Roni grabbed his arm, her eyes pleading. "No, not for this, Dean. This is too private. I'll process it for prints, but please, I don't want everyone to see this."

Dean gave her a look, his brow raised. "What are you saying?"

She couldn't believe he was even considering sharing it, and it came across in her exasperated tone. "I'm saying, go talk to the doorman. Go across the street and check it out, but tell them I thought I saw something, whatever. I'm not inviting the whole team into our private life. Then there's the fact us being together has obviously incensed him. Did this change his kill pattern? I won't get the chance to find out because Mason will ship my ass home as soon as he sees this. I'm on thin ice as it is."

Dean stared at her for a few moments before relenting to her wishes. "One. You get one digression and this is it. And only because my bare ass is involved."

Roni looked again at the negatives before sliding them back into the envelope, her retort saccharin sweet as she glanced at Dean with an arched brow. "But sweetie, that's your best side."

Dean chunked a fortune cookie at her as she ducked in anticipation, her laugh a pleasant change. "I'm going down to get Bristol to walk over with me. I'll call you when I'm headed back. Don't answer the door and don't eat all the ginger chicken."

Pausing at the door he turned and looked at her, his head shaking slowly. "Did you hear anything I said?"

Roni looked up at him with wide, innocent eyes, her fork pausing over the white paper box she'd just opened. "Um, yeah, don't answer the door, eat the chicken. Hurry back and be careful."

Dean growled at her and made her come over to lock the door behind him, drawing her close for a hard kiss before leaving.

✳   ✳   ✳   ✳

Pulling her shirt from her skirt Roni headed to her room to change, her thoughts scattering to the wind when she reached for the light and found her wrist imprisoned. A scream caught in her throat when she was roughly slammed against the wall, the weight of her assailant's body knocking the breath out of her. The split second it would have taken for her to react violently was just enough time for the first syllable to leave his mouth and the sound of his accented voice in her ear turned fear to fury before he finished his sentence. "I thought he'd never leave."

Roni was actually dizzy from the turn of emotions, her retort nearly hissed as she tried to free her wrists, aggravated when his steel like hands easily subdued her efforts. "Do you think that's funny?"

He did actually but he'd never admit it to her. Instead he kissed the pulse throbbing in her neck and lifted his head, not surprised that even in the darkness he could see the rage in her eyes, and he smiled despite it. "I never thought I'd feel your heart beat so fast again ..."

Ignoring the innuendo in his voice, she tried again to free herself and became more frustrated when he didn't let her go. "What are you doing here?"

"I'm not here."

His flippant answer was met by "the sigh," and his attempt to return to the hollow of her neck was met only by stiff resistance. Even with his head warning him not to, Wade still couldn't resist asking, his eyes wandering to her full lips. "Do you love him?"

Roni didn't know if she was more floored by the question or the feelings they evoked; but nevertheless, she didn't like it, and it reflected in her tone. "What do you want?"

Wade shrugged slightly, the dimple in his left cheek deepening with his grin. "A kiss ..."

"Kiss my ass."

Her instantaneous retort made him laugh and she was quick to break his hold, his reflexes not quick enough to dodge the solid jab he received to the stomach for his efforts. "It was a shitty day for you to pull a stunt like that. You scared the bloody hell out of me. And I thought the last time you popped up like this it was supposed to be the last. If they find out you're making contact ..."

Sitting on the edge of her bed, Wade scoffed at her concern over the "policies" of his position. "Are you going to tattle?"

Roni stuck her head out of the closet and looked at him like he'd gone crazy, her short laugh implying that he knew better. "Yeah, right, like I don't have enough trouble with them."

Wade became distracted as she continued undressing while she was speaking, and it was several seconds before he became aware that she was glaring at him expectantly and he realized she was waiting for an answer he didn't have. "Sorry, what?"

Roni sighed dramatically, her retort full of exasperation. "It'd be nice if you'd at least pay attention. I asked you if you have any recall of anyone being overly interested in me in college, if there was anyone you ever noticed watching me."

Wade chuckled softly, his sarcastic reply nothing more than expected. "Other than most of the male student body, no, can't say that I do. But then I did graduate a few years before you. Why, do you think you have a lead?"

She shrugged as she dug through a drawer for a tee shirt. "Maybe, too soon to say."

Grinning at her in the dark, his tone turned teasing. "So can I see the pictures?"

Roni gasped at the thought, her tone turning accusatory. "How do you know about that?"

Wade's brows furrowed in disbelief, his ego wounded at her question. "Oh come now, I know his ways: nasty little notes, intrusive photos.... Is he watching you? I would have looked myself, but the envelope was sealed and I figured you'd get pissy if I opened it." When she glared at him he continued with a heavy sigh. "So it's no then? It's not like I don't know what's going on with you and Colby ..."

"Don't start ..."

There was a hard edge to his tone as he cut her off. "Start what? Reminding you of why you came here, or the consequences your extracurricular activities could have on the outcome of this case?"

Resisting the urge to throw something at him, Roni's reply was barely controlled. "Leave him out of this, Wade. My extracurricular activities, as you call them, have no bearing on this case, and I don't need you or anyone else reminding me of why the hell I'm here. You need to go."

Wade made a sound of disgust, his opinion of Dean coming across loud and clear in his tone. "Why? He'll be across the street chasing his tail for at least twenty more minutes."

Roni bristled at his attitude, quick to defend Dean's abilities. "What's that supposed to mean? Dean's one of the best investigators I've worked with. If there's anything there, he will find it."

Stamping down his jealousy, Wade merely shook his head in a disinterested way, his tone matter-of-fact. "Sorry, I just think he's out of his league here ..."

Roni looked at him like he'd gone daft, suddenly wondering why they were whispering in an empty apartment. "I think you're reaching. Dean can handle anything that this guy can bring."

Dark thoughts preoccupied his mind, making Wade's reply sound hollow. "I guess we'll see about that …"

Sighing heavily she closed the closet and glared at him. "You know, I told Da I didn't want any help. Why are you here?"

"You know why I'm here …"

Roni cut him off in exasperation. "I don't need you here. I have enough protection."

Wade chuckled as he lay back on her bed, the sarcastic humor in his voice not amusing to Roni. "Ummm, yeah, that's why I'm in your bedroom."

He jumped when her palm connected with his stomach, the cynicism in her voice all too familiar to him as she leaned over him. "And you have the technology to bypass the alarm system too, don't you? I'm serious, I don't want you interfering with this investigation. You need to disappear back to wherever you came from."

He shrugged indifferently, his answer ambiguous at best. "But it's nicer here." When she gave him a reproachful look, he sighed heavily, his voice filling with defeat. "I will, I will. I just wanted to make sure you were okay. Your father looked upset when he left …"

"He should have taken you with him …"

Wade fought the anger that welled in his gut but was unsuccessful in schooling his emotions when he abruptly stood. "God, you can be so ungrateful sometimes!"

Roni followed as he turned away, nearly choking on the irony of his remark. "Now you're going to defend him? Defend the lies he's told me my whole life? I'm sick of the deceit and secrets and everything else that goes with his twisted little world of espionage, Wade …"

Which included him, and even as he responded, he chided himself for getting his feelings hurt. He thought he was past those kinds of emotions by now. "Yeah, I know, I got that message with the divorce papers."

Roni stopped by the window he'd used to come in by, her anger easing with his words. She had abandoned him after Emily was murdered, and the guilt she felt now echoed in her softened voice. "I know, and I'm sorry that I screwed us up …"

Wade's soft laugh was full of bitterness, his thoughts in disarray as he checked the streets below to make his exit. "Don't be sorry. Believe me, after the job the Firm has done on me, you're much better off."

Roni shook her head in disbelief as she chuckled at his tone. "You make it sound like they've turned you into a monster."

Wade stopped and looked down at her, the gravity of his words enhanced by the sudden despairing coldness in his eyes. "They have, Roni, make no mistake about that. Countless nights I've held a gun in my hand and tried to stop the madness, but I can't find the courage to pull the trigger …"

Laying a hand on his arm, the naked concern in her voice matched the unease of her gaze. "Wade, don't say.…"

Perturbed by the slip, Wade was quick to deflect her thoughts with a soft chuckle and an improper proposition. "Of course, all you have to do is say the word and I'll take you away and make this nightmare disappear."

Caught off guard by the sudden lust in his eyes, Roni stepped back, her voice gentle as she lowered her gaze. "All of our words have been spoken, Wade."

Wade nodded in resignation, his sigh heavy as he forced a playful tone. "You sure? Last chance before you do something you'll regret."

Roni shook her head in disbelief, giving him a quick hug as he prepared to depart. "I think I'll manage. You though, you'll be careful out there, right?"

Wade chuckled softly as he released her, his voice filling with amusement at the irony of her remark. "You know me and careful aren't on speaking terms, but I'll try."

Once outside the window he knelt to the opening, his hushed voice calling out to her as she started to close the window. "Hey, Roni …"

Roni stopped and leaned out a bit, her tone inquisitive as she looked up at him. "What?"

He shocked her by grabbing her chin and kissing her hard, her parting expletive mingling with his soft laughter as he quietly disappeared up the fire escape. "Dammit, Wade!"

*   *   *   *

Roni barely had time to secure the window and curl up on the couch with the letter her father had left before Dean returned, the disappointment on his face making her question unnecessary. "Didn't find anything?"

Dean shrugged out of his jacket, shaking his head as he took off his shoulder holster and laid it on the entertainment center. "No, there's only one empty apartment on this side of the building and it's clean."

Starting for the kitchen he paused, turning to look at Roni curiously. "Are you okay? You look a little flushed."

Roni choked down the bite of chicken she had just eaten, blurting out the first thing she thought of as she held up the box in her hand for emphasis. "The chicken is spicy tonight."

She laughed at the expression that crossed his face as he walked over and snatched the box from her hand, his outraged tone full of sincerity. "You better not have eaten it all, Donavan."

CHAPTER 9

▼

Dean had barely slept with the thought of that nut watching them, and the more he thought about it the more it bothered him. Pulling into the garage, he waved to the guard as he automatically lifted the gate, absently scanning the area before assisting Roni from the truck, her concerned question throwing him off. "Are you okay?"

"Huh?"

His preoccupation was making her nervous and she stopped in her tracks, speaking this time with a little more concern in her tone. "I said, are you okay? You haven't had ten words to say to me all morning. What's wrong?"

Dean rolled his neck, trying to release the tension that had been building all night, and forced a smile as he prodded her toward the elevator. "Yeah, sorry, it's just really starting to bug me. I have the impression that this guy considers you to be cheating on him, and that he thinks of you in that way is enough to keep me awake at night. But to know he probably sat there and watched us make love through a camera just really pisses me off."

Roni waited for the elevator doors to close before responding to his burst of possessiveness. "It's just part of his game. It gives him a weird sense of control. But if he's jealous of you, it's only because you draw my attention away from him, and away from the investigation. Statistically speaking, he's probably impotent and a loser with women."

Dean's hand went around her waist as he turned her toward him, his eyes suddenly bright with interest. "Do you think he'll come after me?"

Laughing softly she shook her head, stretching up on her toes to kiss him softly. "I don't know, but don't sound so excited about it; because if he did, he wouldn't play fair."

The look that possessed his eyes was unfamiliar to her, a cold, hard look that matched the edge in his voice. "What makes you think *I* would?"

The elevator dinged and they separated, the doors opening to find Mason standing there looking impatient. His smile was instantaneous upon seeing them. "There you are. I was headed downstairs to see if you had stopped by the lab."

Roni glanced at a silent Dean. Their tardiness was mostly his fault, but she couldn't tell Mason that, so she fibbed. "I had some computer problems this morning. Took me a bit to get the bugs knocked out."

Mason nodded at her double meaning, taking her by the elbow to steer them toward the control room. "The books arrived this morning and we took the liberty of starting. Already, we have some solid leads." Roni smiled at him. His enthusiasm was quite a change from his usual staunchness. Stepping down into the control room, they took their seats at the table and settled in while Tyler loaded up his findings and an intern poured the coffee.

Mason sat back in his chair with his steaming cup, nodding to Tyler. "Go ahead."

Ty looked up at the screen, his tired eyes telling their tale: he had been there all night following electronic trails across the Internet and into sundry files." He took a deep breath as the pictures started popping up. "Okay, we have found in our travels that there were 125 applicants to the Sherlock Society and 30 chosen. Out of the 95 remaining applicants, there were 10 applicants that applied more than twice. These are those ten."

Lyn leaned forward, her eyes studying the faces popping up on the screen. "Roni, how do they apply?"

"You submit a scenario and they choose the teams based on the best ones." Roni stared up at the faces, wishing one of them looked familiar, but they didn't. "I don't know any of them."

Looking at the yearbooks, Dean had already begun to notice a pattern. Studying the pictures in the section on the varsity games, he found that Roni was either in every picture itself or in the background. "Roni, did you know the yearbook photographer? A friend, perhaps?"

Roni shook her head, her brows knitting. "No, I remember there always being photographers on the field, from the papers and yearbooks, but I didn't really know any of them."

Dean handed Ty the book, his brow raised. "Can you scan these two pages?"

Ty smiled broadly as he took the book from him, thriving with the prospect of playing with his new toys. "Considering my new scanner handles larger files, yes I can. Thank you, Mason."

Mason gave him a slight nod as he smiled behind his coffee cup. "No problem, Tyler, you deserve it."

Ty grinned as he scanned the pages, making room for Dean as he slid over to mark the shots he wanted highlighted. "Every picture on this page has you in it some way or another." Ty was already on Dean's track, and before they could ask, the picture of the photographer popped up on top of the yearbook spread.

"Photo credits belong to Nicholas Harris, yearbook photographer. Shot the games for two years. Applied only once to the society, but was not chosen. He didn't make our first cut because he didn't match the profile." Roni took a shuddering breath, the face staring back at her vaguely familiar as she told them why. "Because he was American, he was a loner, a nerd. The society council made fun of him, called him 'Icky Nicky,' but I never participated in that." She looked up at Dean with a resigned sigh, her head shaking slowly. "He hid behind the camera. No one ever paid him any mind."

Ty looked up at her, his smile smug. "I guess not, seeing as he was in your Russian history class for two semesters and has a degree in botany."

Looking at the old familiar pages splayed upon the wall, she shook her head in disbelief, her voice full of awe. "I can't believe I didn't notice that."

Mason was quick to defend her intelligence. "I don't think anyone would notice it unless they were looking for it. How many times do you look at a group shot and notice the people in the background?"

Lyn nodded in agreement to Mason's observation. "I think you're right. It's a very subtle obsession. He's very meticulous, very controlling ..."

Tyler's excited exclamation interrupted her analogy, his smile broad. "And he's employed by a photography company based out of Denver. His current position? Taking high school photographs. He's worked there for over six months now."

Lyn's brow shot up as she looked at Roni. "That's how he find's them. Ask a few questions, take a few pictures, a teenage girl doesn't think twice about telling someone when her birthday is or where she lives."

Ty held up a finger as Mason opened his mouth to ask, already pulling the address from his application. "1184 Birch Cove, Apartment D."

Roni shook her head, the exasperation coming out in her voice. "No, it's too easy; and he's not killing these girls in an apartment."

Mason stood and gathered his notepads, his voice firm. "Need I remind anyone how many people Dahmer killed in his apartment? I'll work on the search warrant. Lyn, Dean, be ready to roll in half an hour." Even as Roni opened her mouth to verbally protest being left behind, he shut her down. "No. If it's necessary, you can go back to the scene after its secured, but not before."

Dean gave her a wink as he prepared to leave, his voice full of teasing. "Oh, stop pouting. You're not that kind of agent, remember?"

She glared at him, still angry at being left behind. "Oh, shut up."

Dean chuckled, resisting the urge to kiss her pouting lips as he moved to leave. Stopping on the landing to answer his phone, his world as he knew it crashed to a halt with his sister's frantic words. "Dean, Steph's missing ..."

His response brought Roni out of her chair and to his side. "What do you mean, 'Steph's missing'?" What proceeded was an emotional outpouring of words that Dean couldn't understand, and frustration made his response seem harsh. "I can't understand a damn thing you're saying, Carol. Calm down and tell me what's happened."

Roni snatched his phone from him, her reprimand going practically unheard by Dean's buzzing ears. "Screaming at her won't help." Taking a breath, she pushed her emotions aside and addressed Carol with a calm voice. "Carol, it's Roni. When was the last time Stephanie was seen, and who was she with?"

Hearing the commotion, Mason returned to the room, his gaze full of concern as he looked from Dean's ashen face to Tyler's. "What's going on?"

Watching Dean pace for a second, Tyler swallowed the lump in his throat and answered, almost wishing their tight family atmosphere didn't give him the ability to do so. "His niece is missing. Roni's talking to his sister now ..."

Mason muttered an oath and sigh heavily, his voice reassuring as he stopped Dean's pacing. "You think it's related?"

"Yes, it is."

They all turned to look at Roni's pale face, her hand covering the phone as she relayed the bad news. "A classmate says he saw a man wrestling Stephanie into a dark-colored van, but by the time he could get to her, they were gone. The man left one rose in the street."

Sighing over Dean's oath, Mason started adjusting his plans. "I'll call and get a rush on the warrant ..."

Dean turned toward the door with an angry stride, his tone causing Mason to physically step into his path. "Screw the warrant ..."

With a hand on his chest and a tone that denied argument, Mason put his foot down, hoping beyond all else that Dean had too much respect for him to put him on his ass. "You're not putting all of our hard work, Veronica's hard work, down the drain by running off half-cocked. Slow down, find out some facts, and let me get this done right."

"I promised them they would be safe. Mason!"

"Slow down."

Dean took a breath and gave Mason a short nod, his anger dissipating when he looked at Roni and saw the silent tears coursing down her cheeks. Her strength for Carol never wavered as she talked to her in a composed, confident voice. "We're going to get her back, I promise. He did this because he knows how close we are and he's trying to up the stakes; but we've got him, Carol. We've identified him, and it won't be long before a team of agents closes in on him."

Dean squatted beside her chair, squeezing her shoulder for support as he thought of the quickest way to get Carol and Jason to Denver. "Tell her to leave Matty and Griffin with Bill, and I'll send a chopper for them."

Roni nodded her head, wiping away tears with the back of her hand as she handed him the phone. "She's already made arrangements for the boys. She's ready …"

Dean turned when Mason called from the doorway, his previous comment for his sister forgotten as he rushed her off the phone and hurried after Mason. "They're on the way, Sis. Roni will be here waiting on you."

The room was quiet for several moments before Tyler spoke in a concerned tone as he pushed a box of tissue across the table to Roni. "You okay?"

Roni grabbed a handful of tissues as she rose from her chair, her response anguished as she hurried towards the exit. "She's not in that apartment, Ty."

*   *   *   *

Roni made a straight path to the lab, praying on the way that her gut hunch research program she'd left running had turned up something. Just knowing that they were wasting time going to the address Harris had provided was killing her. Time was running out and they needed a break, for Stephanie's sake.

The thing that had been nagging at her the most was his message to her, "I knew you'd come home to me." The surface meaning was there, but to her it went deeper. The statement insinuated she had a "home" in Denver. With that thought Roni had started a program to run all possible combinations of her name; and now, sitting behind the computer, her heart was in her throat as she began searching the results. Halfway down the list the mouse stilled, her lip catching in her teeth in concentration. An archive file had culled a listing of a residence for Roark Finnegan, which, coincidently enough, was the only alias of her father's that she knew. Tapping a finger on the mouse, she contemplated her options. She knew what she wanted to do, but did she have the guts to do it?

Walking to the rain-streaked window, she stared out at the glowing lights of downtown Denver and let her mind wander. Should she call Dean, wait on the team? Should she go alone? Was it even relevant information? The many "ifs" still didn't ease the troublesome feeling in her stomach, and with a glance at her watch she made a decision, be it rash or not. "Screw it."

Crossing the room she opened a cabinet and dragged out her backpack, carrying it into Juni's office and closing the blinds. Finding her gym gear, she dressed quickly in a black running suit, securing the laces on her dark-colored sneakers before pocketing cash, Dean's business card, and an ancient pick kit. For many years the kit had been junk in her bag, but today she was glad to have the tools. Donning a lab coat to cover her clothing, her resolve was firm as she left the office and walked out of the FBI building through the morgue bay.

$$*\qquad*\qquad*\qquad*$$

"This is it."

Roni jumped at the cabbie's rough voice, her own sounding foreign to her ears as she urged him to pull up a little. She stared at the house through the rain-streaked pane, her attention drawn back to the man when he cleared his throat and addressed her in gruff exasperation. "You gettin' out or what?"

Roni sat forward to pay, holding up a bill as she leveled him with a stare. "There's an extra twenty in it for you if you make a phone call for me." When he started to balk, Roni reached into her pocket and handed him Dean's card, the seriousness of her tone and the FBI emblem on the card capturing his attention. "Just call and give him this address. That's all you have to do." He took the twenty from her, surprising her by pulling out a mobile and beginning to dial the number. Muttering a thank you, Roni shrugged out of her lab coat and climbed out of the cab, her rash decision to check into this herself not sounding like a good idea now that she was standing there without backup, or even a gun.

With a deep breath she squinted through the rain and started for the semi dark house sitting back off the street, stooping down to creep around the darkest side. Her heart stopped when she saw a little greenhouse attached to the garage, and she had to make the decision then on whether to carry on or retreat and wait for backup. One thought of Stephanie being inside and she continued around the house to look for a way in, the whole time wondering what she would do if she were wrong. What if there was some old couple in there having dinner?

She lucked out to find an unlocked window hidden by overgrown hedges on the rear side of the house. With her size, she had no problem squeezing through the underbrush and through the window. Once inside she crouched in the corner of the dark room and let her eyes adjust to the light and her ears adjust to the noises of the house. She could hear the muffled volume of a television somewhere in the house but not much of anything else. Standing slowly she looked around the room, noticing it was practically empty except for a bed and a chest. She lowered the window to a crack and crossed to the door, her movements silent and calculated as she opened the door and peered into the hallway. All was dark and clear. Four steps down the hall and she heard her. There was a small, scared, whimpering sound coming from behind one of the closed doors off of the corridor. Okay, so there was no little old couple in there eating chicken pot pies.

She had to find out where Harris was first. She was pretty sure he wasn't in the room with Stephanie and she had to pinpoint his location before she tried anything. Hearing a door open, she pressed herself against the wall, holding her breath for what seemed like forever before she was sure he wasn't headed her way. Creeping to the doorway of the kitchen, she peeked around the frame to see the basin full of flowers. She couldn't see them clearly but they looked like cannas. Try as she might, she couldn't remember Stephanie's birthday.

Roni would never understand the psyche of a man that could kill without a single moral thought. But by the way his gear was laid out on the kitchen table, Harris was about to send the FBI a new present. With slow movements she retreated and withdrew the lock-picking tool she had brought, her ear tuned to Harris' every sound as she tried the door to the room. She was shocked to find it wasn't locked, until she got a look inside.

Stephanie was huddled in the center of the bed, her soft weeping masking Roni's entrance into the room. The windows and walls were covered with black plastic, the darkness masking the pieces of paper littering the walls. She figured they were pictures, probably torment for his victims, along with the smell. The sound of metal scraping metal alerted Roni that Stephanie was cuffed to the bed frame, and she hoped she could still pick a lock in a timely manner. Moving quietly to her side, Stephanie's gasp was the only indication that Roni had been detected, and her voice was urgent and hushed. "Stephanie, it's me. I'm going to get you out of here, sweetheart."

Roni could hear the fear in her voice, could smell blood on her breath, as she hissed at her. "You're crazy. He'll kill us both."

Roni grabbed her hands for reassurance, her tone urgent. "Shhhh, be quiet, we're going a few doors down to an empty room and out the window. Now try to hold still while I pick this lock."

Stephanie nodded silently as tears flowed from her eyes. Her uncle wasn't there tearing the door down with a team of agents, which meant Roni was alone, and nuts. But right now she would take nuts if it meant saving her life.

Roni had never been so thankful to be talented at picking locks, and she silently thanked her ex-husband when she felt the chamber click. Helping Stephanie to her feet she gave her a second to gather herself before leading her to the door. With a finger to her lips, she eased the door open and checked the hallway, slipping out to check on Harris' whereabouts. Though she couldn't see him, she could still hear him moving about in the kitchen.

Focusing her priorities she went back and quietly pulled Stephanie from her hiding spot and pushed her down the hall in front of her, glancing over her shoulder every time the sound of the TV broke between commercials. By the time they made it to the window her heart was pounding so loud that she was sure he would be able to hear it at the other end of the house.

Sliding open the old wooden window she grimaced as it shuddered a bit, but Stephanie's gasp was much worse. Fearing detection Roni almost shoved her out the window, her instructions brief and urgent. "Push through the shrubs and run like hell."

Stephanie paused, her voice quiet. "What about you?"

Giving her a nudge, Roni smiled, "I'm right behind you."

Stephanie squeezed out between the house and the bushy shrubs that hid the window, her hand tightly holding onto Roni's to help her out. Roni had one leg out of the window and was ducking down to go through when pain burst through her skull. Crying out, she immediately reached for her ponytail, responding to Stephanie's terrified shriek. "Run, Steph!"

Her second reaction was to free herself from the wicked hold Harris had on her. But after a minute of scuffling in the dark, he punched her in the face, hard. After two more attempts to overcome him, she ended up being dragged halfway down the hall; so she stopped, saving her energy for another opportunity. When he kicked open the door of the room she'd freed Stephanie from, she knew what he intended. But when he flipped on the light and she actually saw the interior, she stumbled, hitting the floor hard as he threw her forward. The walls, streaked with blood splatter from his victims, were plastered with pictures—pictures of all of his victims, before and after, pictures of her that spanned over years of her life, of her family and her friends. How had the Security Service let this happen? And how had she not known someone was so obsessed with her? With a shuddering breath she closed her eyes against the crime scene they had looked so hard for. Five girls had been killed here, and she was about to become the sixth.

Pain exploded in her face and she realized he had slapped her, his fingers digging into her flesh as he snatched her chin back around to face him.

"Dammit, Veronica, look at me when I'm talking to you! Why did you do that? Why would you go and ruin everything I had planned? Do you know how hard I worked for this moment? This is not how you were supposed to find out!"

Blood ran from her lip as she focused in on him, pain dulling her senses as relief clashed with fear, confusion heavy in her barely audible whisper. "Wade?"

Wade laughed in light of her confusion. He wished he had a picture of the look on her face; it was so priceless. "Yes, princess. Who'd you expect? I can't believe you actually think I'd let Harris live after ruining my life. That psycho was dead a week after the Waltham chit was killed."

Roni tried to shake the pain out of her head, the absurdity of the situation making the denial thick in her voice as she attempted to stand. "No, you couldn't ..."

Wade roughly hauled her to her feet and slammed her against the wall, the rest of her thought dissipating in a cloud of pain as he unleashed the fury that'd been festering inside him. "I couldn't *what*? Kill? Maim? Torture? I've done a lot of things I never thought I could do; the system made sure of that. They knew he did it, Roni, but they'd sit back and let Harris kill over and over again. You know why? Because it makes the world afraid and diverts attention away from the real monsters: people like me, and your father." Roni tried to turn her head away from the hatred in his eyes, but he wouldn't let her, the punishing arm across her neck pressing her head harder against the wall. "I killed him for you, Roni, so you'd quit chasing him and come back to me, but you wouldn't stop. You kept on and on until I had no choice but to become what you loved: a murderer."

Anger flared in her eyes, her response a near hiss as some of her spirit returned. "You bastard! Don't you dare say you did this for me."

A hard jerk and her head struck the wall with a numbing thud, Wade's voice shaking with emotion. "You ungrateful bitch! Since the day I laid eyes on you, everything I've done has been for you. Do you think I wanted to join the SIS, Roni? Do you care that my soul was damned after my very first 'assignment'? I've lied, cried, killed, and even died for you, but you were too self-absorbed to see it! You're always too busy trying to show your father how smart you are."

Stepping backward Wade let her slide to the floor, his tone mocking as he squatted in front of her. "And for what? That manipulating bastard doesn't care as long as he's got you in his control. I had to show you how far he'd go, Roni. You wouldn't have believed me if I hadn't proved it to you. He withheld valuable information while a killer ran loose, because he couldn't find the evidence. Well, I found it, didn't I? I found it for you ..."

When he leaned forward to touch her cheek, she reacted, taking advantage of the momentary softening of his eyes. With a hard sweep she took his feet from under him and got two steps away before he tripped her. Trying to kick herself free, the terror in her heart made her plea more desperate. "Oh God, Wade, what's happened to you?"

What petrified her most of all was that she knew the man attacking her wasn't the man she'd married. This man was a machine, a heartless, emotionless, killing machine. After struggling with him for what seemed like forever, she knew only that she'd got three solid punches in before she felt the cord wrap around her throat, and that's when fear consumed her like never before.

Sheer force slammed her backward against his chest and the air left her in a loud gust as she pulled desperately at his hands, his words a spiteful breath against her ear. "I should have known you wouldn't appreciate what I've done for you, you who devoted yourself to a man who's lied to you your entire life. Through it all I was the one who stood by you, supported you, and in the end, it was I who gave you what you wanted most. I gave you a career without your father's involvement, and this is what I get in return?"

Roni tried to breathe as the cord got tighter and tighter, and even through the pounding in her ears, she could still hear the disappointment in his voice, the pain and rejection in his mad whispers. "I worked so hard to earn your love, Veronica ..."

Spots blurred her vision seconds before the blackness consumed her.

*   *   *   *

Stephanie ignored the branches scratching her arms and the rocks digging in her feet, and did what Roni said: she ran like hell. Around the side of the house and across the yard, her prayers were answered as a swarm of vehicles screeched to a halt with their lights flashing. Running to the first man with a FBI windbreaker on, she wasn't surprised to see her uncle and she grabbed his arm in a vise-like grip, sheer panic in her voice. "You have to hurry, Dean. He's going to kill her!"

Dean drew his gun as he pushed Stephanie toward Lyn, her arm protectively going around the girl's shoulders as Mason started shouting at him to wait. Dean heard the command, but for the first time in his life, he disobeyed a direct order, his one and only goal being to get to Roni, drag her out of the house, and whip her ass for taking off like she did.

Opting for the back door, he skirted around the side of the house, noting both the van in the garage and the adjoining greenhouse before creeping onto the back porch. With a quick prayer for patience and accuracy, he eased the door open, his ears straining for any sound to give away their location inside.

It took only seconds for him to recognize the sound of Roni choking and fewer for him to react. Three steps down the hall he swung into the doorway, his eyes meeting hers just before they rolled back and her head fell forward, exposing the smug face of her killer, his spiteful words slicing Dean to the bone.

"Now no one gets the whor ..."

Wade's mocking remark was interrupted by the bullet that pierced his forehead and left his insult unfinished.

Lurching forward Dean caught Roni's body before she hit the floor, cradling her against him as he turned and carried her out of there. Alive or dead, he would not let her spend one more second in that house. Kneeling over her at the bottom of the back steps, he checked her pulse and started CPR, his heart pounding so hard that he did not hear Mason barking orders to the medics that had arrived. Stopping his compressions, he checked her pulse again, a sob catching in his throat as he leaned down to give her another breath. "Come on, baby. Breathe!"

Two minutes later he was railing at her, the fear of losing her angering him. "God damn it, breathe!"

Mason was moving in to forcibly remove him so they could defibrillate her heart when she gasped, and he froze, waiting for her next movement. Dean's hands stilled over her ribs until the next breath came, a wash of relief nearly crumpling his composure when she started coughing.

It wasn't until then that Dean realized there were at least a dozen people surrounding him in the rain, their collective sighs echoing his sentiment as he lifted her from the ground to put her on the waiting gurney.

Roni started coming around in the ambulance, disorientation making her lash out before Dean got her calmed down enough to get an oxygen mask on her. Holding her hand, he looked up at her muffled question, the blown vessels in her eyes a testament to how close they'd come to losing her. "Is she okay?"

Shaking his head in disbelief he leaned over to push the damp hair away from her face, his eyes misting despite his brave front. "Yeah, but you won't be when I kick your ass for not waiting on me."

Roni squeezed his hand, her eyes closing against the pain that began to manifest throughout her body, her whispered retort actually wringing a chuckle out of him. "You can try, Cowboy."

CHAPTER 10

▼

Sitting on the side of the bed, Roni, unseeing, flipped the channels on the television, annoyed that she had been there for hours while everyone else was working her crime scene. She was going mad sitting there repeatedly going over things in her head. She was angry, hurt, and confused. She wanted some answers, and her answers were in that house. Hell, besides being sore, her only true discomforts were an extremely tender throat and a killer headache. She didn't care what they said, she was a doctor and she was leaving, just as soon as someone got past Satan's nurses. Hearing Dean's voice outside the door, she turned off the television and sat up straighter, her spirits automatically lifting. As the door opened she started off the bed, only to be stopped by Dean's reproachful look and stern rebuke.

"Get your ass back in bed. You're not going anywhere tonight. Overnight observation, Roni, and quit giving these people hell about it. I don't know who is worse, you or Stephanie."

Her expression was one of disagreement, but from the sound of her voice, even she didn't blame them for being worried. "Boy, they didn't waste any time ratting me out, did they? How is she?"

Reaching out to smooth her bangs from her eyes, he was amazed by her concern for another. In light of her condition and the circumstances that had brought her there, he'd expected her to be a hysterical mess. "She's okay. I left her sleeping under the watchful eyes of her parents. Carol tried to come by earlier, but they wouldn't let her in to see you. She sends her love and gratitude." Before she could respond, Dean cupped her cheek and pulled her close for a tender kiss, his voice softening. "There's my gratitude, and the rest you get once you're better."

Roni grinned at the promise in his tone, the coarseness of her voice unable to mar the effect her whispered reply had on him. "Mmm, I'm better already …"

Too many emotions flooded his brain and Dean found himself tearing up as he rested his forehead on hers, his apology barely audible. "I'm sorry …"

Roni stopped him with a finger to the lips, and although she was unable to stop the tears that blurred her vision, gave him a courageous smile. "Don't. I wouldn't be alive if it weren't for you." Taking a breath, her smile went a little devilish as she tried to lighten him up. "I'm fine, Dean. Other than the ribs you bruised giving me CPR, really, I'm okay."

As hard as it was for him, Dean pushed her away, his threat given only half jokingly as she chuckled at him. "Yeah, but you won't be after I kick your ass, you insubordinate."

Juni's voice interrupted as she and Lyn entered the room, her tone full of amusement. "Won't be what?"

Dean gave Roni a withering look as he stepped out of Juni's way, his tone one of exaggerated disbelief. "She says she's okay."

Juni snorted as she grabbed Roni's chin and lifted her head up to look at the purple-red marks across her throat. "You aren't okay. Should I list the complications that could occur with disrupted oxygen flow to the brain? Not to mention the brutal blows you took to the head. Good thing that's hard as a rock."

Roni made a face at her while the others laughed. If Juni kept up she'd be in the hospital for a week. "Okay, okay, you win. I'll be good. Don't pick on me. I've had a bad day."

Juni grinned in spite of Roni's pout, giving her an impromptu hug. "That's a good girl." Sobering completely, her gaze filled with empathy. "I'm sorry, Roni, I don't think anyone saw this coming, and I can't imagine what you've been through. But I'll tell you one thing, after getting a good look at that room, I'm very relieved you're alive."

Roni nodded in agreement, her voice laced with doubt as she looked up at Dean. "I'm a bit thankful myself. I think I was in denial right up until I lost consciousness, and I'm still spinning trying to sort things out."

Dean shrugged lightly as he leaned against the wall. "What's to sort out? Harris killed to get your attention and Donavan used Harris. He knew you'd follow him here. The girls were just a pawn in his twisted game to keep you under his idea of control."

Making an unladylike sound, Lyn's observation was full of sarcasm as she grinned at Dean. "Are you bucking for my job, or what?"

Nudging Juni to the side, Lyn gave Roni a hug, her tone supportive as she took her hands. "None of this matters right now. You don't need to be worrying about anything tonight, Roni. You need to rest. And while I'm nagging, you know this case has consumed so much of your time that it may take you a while to adjust to the 'over' part of it, so don't rush it. You're going to have to be patient." When Roni nodded absently, Lyn gave her a pointed look, visions of that horrible room invading her thoughts. "Promise that you'll talk to someone about this, Roni. Don't let it fester …"

Understanding her concern, Roni nodded, her eyes dropping to the hospital blanket balled up in her fist. "I will."

Juni pulled on Lyn's sleeve to get her attention, her voice teasing. "Geez, didn't ya hear the girl? She's had a tough day. Leave her alone." Laughing off Juni's chiding, she gave Roni one more hug, her voice filling with sincerity as she prepared to leave. "We're going to get out of here so you can rest. We just wanted to stop by to make sure you were okay."

Roni nodded slightly, her smile earnest as she responded. "I'm fine, really. I appreciate you guys coming because I know Mason will have you back at work at the break of dawn."

Pausing at the door, Lyn gave her a knowing look, her tone one of disdain. "I wish. He gave us leave to come see you and now it's back to work, but he'll be glad to hear you're up and argumentative already."

Dean's laugh was short and hard as he pushed from the wall, his parting remark for Lyn getting him the look from Roni. "You mean 'as usual.'"

Lyn laughed as she eyed him with a raised brow, her tone chiding as she departed. "Oh, you're so asking for it …"

Dean chuckled as he shrugged out of his jacket and started rolling up his sleeves, and Roni couldn't help but grin to see that he would be staying with her. "You don't have to stay anymore, you know?"

Dean cut her a look, the seriousness of his tone making her giggle. "Don't be trying to get out of your punishment. You know you deserve it."

Motioning for him to join her on the bed, her thoughts turned serious as he got comfortable. Stifling a yawn, she leaned against him and tried to appease her curiosity. "Yeah, I know I do. What happened in there, Dean?"

Dean reached out and gingerly touched the purpling bruise on her cheekbone, a tinge of anger lingering in his voice. "I could ask you the same thing. For my part, Stephanie ran from the house screaming he was killing you, and when I came through the door and saw your face, saw how white you were, I thought you were dead. All I could think was that we were too late." He took a deep breath and exhaled slowly, his voice quiet. "You went limp and he smirked at me like he'd just won the grand prize, and I killed him. I didn't realize until afterwards who it was."

Roni leaned up to kiss him, her eyes full of sincerity. "Thank you for saving my life, Dean. It was really stupid of me to think I could handle the situation alone, then to be blindsided like that. You were right, you know. It's a little different when someone's willing to kill you."

Dean cupped her face in his hands, his heart breaking at the look in her eyes. "Stephanie doesn't think your stupid, and neither do I. Impulsive, reckless, brave, and insubordinate, but never stupid."

Roni smiled through tears and Dean gathered her in his arms, kissing the top of her head as he thought of the night's events. If he had waited as Mason had instructed him, she would be dead right now. It had been a matter of seconds that had saved her; and for all they knew, the same had been true for Stephanie. Feeling her slump against him, Dean planted another kiss on her forehead, grinning as the sedative Juni had slipped into her I.V. took full effect.

Forewarned that Roni had refused medication, Dean had left both Lyn and Juni arguing with the head nurse to give them the meds. Personally, he didn't think they had a chance and was surprised to see Juni with it; but nevertheless, he was thankful because she wouldn't be sleeping tonight, not without aid. With a heavy sigh he leaned back and gazed down at her, his hand shaking as he smoothed a tendril of hair from her cheek. The emotions he'd experienced in the last few hours were disturbing and unusual to him, and he didn't quite know how to handle them. Laying his chin on her head, he closed his eyes knowing only one thing for certain: his world wasn't going to be right again for a very long time.

*   *   *   *

Dean woke to a gentle hand on his shoulder, the calm authoritative tone of the man's accented voice making an introduction unnecessary. "Go find some coffee, son." Nodding obediently, Dean pulled his tired body from the chair beside Roni's bed and shrugged into his jacket as he stifled a yawn and headed for the door. "Colby?"

Stopping, he turned as Roni's father looked up from his daughter's sleeping face, the gratitude in his eyes far more than that in his voice. "Thank you." With a simple nod Dean left them, going first to find coffee, then family of his own to check on.

Waking to the sound of her father's voice had Roni even more confused, and it took her a few seconds to comprehend his presence. Her brow furrowed for the briefest of moments before the nights' events flooded her brain and sent her into his embrace a bawling idiot.

With a heavy sigh Finn fought the overwhelming sense of relief, glad for the opportunity to hold her tightly and assure himself that she was indeed all right. As much as he'd been through in his life, he couldn't remember a more upsetting phone call, and even as quickly as he'd arrived in the States, it still hadn't been fast enough for him.

It was moments later when father and daughter parted, and Roni's voice was a weakened whisper as she fought a new wave of tears. "You're here for him?"

Finn gave her hands a squeeze, his voice reassuring as he leaned forward to capture her full gaze. "Considering the circumstances, yes, but I never should have left you here to begin with either. We'll leave for the airfield as soon as you're discharged."

The thought of leaving nearly sent her into a panic and her grasp on his hands tightened as tears streaked her cheeks and she choked out her plea. "Please, Da, I can't. Just give me a few days, okay?"

Taking a deep breath, Finn was about to be the ogre and tell her no when a picture flashed in his brain and he changed his mind. After the recap he'd been given, the last thing he'd expected to see when he walked into her room was Dean Colby slouched in a bedside chair—his chosen place beside his daughter, although his niece was admitted to the same hospital. There was more here to clean up than the mess he'd volunteered to handle and Roni was the only one to do it. "I'll send you an itinerary when I get back."

Roni barely nodded in response, her voice cracking as she looked at him warily. "What happened to him, Da?"

It was the question Finn had been dreading the most, but only because he knew the answer and was partly responsible for this outcome. His gaze dropped as he cleared his throat nervously. "It seems I owe you another apology. They called months ago and told me Wade was missing in the field and was presumed dead, but with everything else going on I didn't want to tell you. I kept hoping he'd show up again." Taking a breath, his tone softened and Roni thought he sounded a bit remorseful when he continued. "He was pushed to the inside too quickly, had too much put on him too fast. When you two started having problems, I told him to give you space, to concentrate on his work and let you work things out in your own way. Unfortunately for him, your way was divorce and I'm sure he thought I influenced it, just as he thought I influenced his career ..."

"You didn't?"

Finn smiled at her suspicious tone, expecting nothing less from her. "No actually, he excelled there all by himself. However, there lies the problem. When someone shows a specific aptitude, especially Wade's type, it's hard at times to know whether or not it should be nurtured. You can test and train all you want, but until an agent is put into the grind, you never know how they'll handle the pressure put on them."

Roni nodded thoughtfully, reflecting on Wade's visit the prior week. "He came to see me the night you were here. I see now he was fishing for information; but at the time, I assumed he was with you."

Trying to gain a little insight into Wade's actions, Finn was careful with his questions. "Did you argue? Did he give you any reason to suspect ...?"

Roni's laugh was full of bitterness, her voice full of hurt. "When did we ever have a conversation that didn't end in an argument? But no, I never got the impression he wanted to kill me."

Finn raised a hand to smooth her hair from her cheek, his reply full of resignation. "It doesn't matter anymore, honey; he won't hurt you or anyone else again. The best thing for you would be to try and put all of this behind you ..."

Roni pulled away from him with a thoughtful frown, suddenly awash with suspicion as Wade's words echoed in her brain. "Did the SIS know who Emily's murderer was? You know much of what Wade did was meant to enlighten me about the corruption of our family, to show me that I would be better with him than listening to you, someone who has misled me my whole life ..."

Finn immediately went on the defensive, his hand rising to stop her tirade. "Whoa there, lass, everything I've ever done, every lie I've ever told you or anyone in this family has only been to keep you safe ..."

"For our protection, yes I've heard. And how safe do you think I feel right now, Da? How trusting do you think I am of your 'people'?"

Finn stood in frustration, muttering an oath as he walked to the window. "This is why your brothers are on the fire brigade, Veronica. You put me in these impossible situations and expect me to be open when you know ..."

"You can't." The acceptance in her voice turned him back towards her as she continued. "I don't know why I fight it. I know the policies because not only has it been my entire life, but I signed a confidentiality contract just like you did. It just hurts to think that all of this could have been averted had Nicholas Harris been properly incarcerated last year."

The raw pain in his gaze was a rare glimpse into his torment, his carefully emphasized words full of meaning. "Knowing and proving are two different things. I was trying to collect enough evidence of Harris' involvement when he disappeared. When he reentered the United States, the decision was made not to pursue him, and that mistake I will carry with me till my dying day. But it's also my burden to carry, and mine alone. Understand?"

Roni merely nodded in response, the power of his words lingering with her for long after he had left. She would not promise him because she could not help the guilt that weighted her heart, but it was somewhat a relief to know that there was someone else carrying a share.

*   *   *   *

When the door opened next, Roni was in the process of getting out of bed, Dean's look of reprimand as far as he got before Stephanie bounded from the wheelchair behind him and literally tackled Roni with a hug, her exuberant greeting making her laugh. "Oh my God, you are by far either the bravest or the craziest woman I've ever met. I can't believe you came into that maniac's house alone. Thank God you're okay!"

Hearing her voice, Roni looked up at Carol over the teenager's head, the unshed tears in her eyes weighting her casual comment as she walked toward the bed. "I echo Stephanie's sentiments."

Coloring slightly, Roni's laugh was soft as she looked toward Dean. "At least everyone agrees that I'm crazy."

It had taken only seconds for Dean to realize Roni had been crying, and knowing why, he ignored her comment and gave her a little nod, his question heavy with meaning. "Are you okay?"

Even as her eyes welled with tears she gave him a valiant smile, glad that her voice sounded more confident than she felt. "Yeah, I'm fine."

Standing at her bedside, Carol reached out and gave her shoulder a squeeze, her heartfelt words touching Roni's heart. "I know there's no way we can repay you for what you did, but if there's ever a time you need us, please know that Jason and I consider you part of our family."

Struggling to voice a response over the lump in her throat, she laughed when Stephanie saved her the trouble, her observation full of sarcasm as she pushed away from Roni and glared at her mother. "Gee, Mom, you're supposed to reward her, not punish her."

Giving her daughter a good-natured shove, Carol reprimanded her in jest. "That'll be enough out of you, prissy."

Stephanie made a face at her mother, her expression turning somber when she looked back at Roni. She was still struggling to understand why Roni had done what she had for her, puzzled by the risk she had taken for someone she hardly knew. "Why'd you do it? Weren't you scared?"

Roni reached out and tucked a strand of hair behind Stephanie's ear, and then answered her candidly. "Yes, I was, but no matter how scared I was, I knew you were inside even more terrified than I was." Taking a breath she looked pointedly at Dean, the conviction in her words making his stomach lurch. "And too, because I knew if Dean arrived and forced a confrontation, that you wouldn't leave that house alive, and I couldn't let that happen." When he gave her a nod of resignation, she gave him a small grin, her tone void of humor. "I told you he wouldn't fight fair."

Fighting off the panic that rolled in her gut, Carol took a steady breath and tried to change the subject, her invitation genuinely given. "Well, I'm just glad it's over and that you're both all right. Roni, I don't know what your plans are now, but we'd love for you to come to the ranch for a week or two, until you're back on your feet."

Roni reached out and squeezed her hand as she smiled, thinking of her family as she politely declined. "Carol, I'm fine, really. I plan on returning to the Bureau when I'm released, and when I'm finished there I have to go back home. I've already put my father off once and I have an upset family to soothe as well, but I truly appreciate the invitation. I'm sorry I can't accept."

Carol felt like an idiot for not considering her family. If Roni's mother knew the details then there wasn't any doubt that she was beyond anxious to see for herself that her daughter was okay. "I understand. I'm sure they are anticipating your return. How about a rain check? You can come back for a vacation whenever you want."

Even if it was only a thought she kept in the back of her mind, Roni grasped at the opportunity to return. "That would be great."

Both women turned toward Stephanie when she spoke, her strained question intensified by the silent tears that streaked her cheeks. "You promise? You'll really come back?"

Roni was shocked by her distress and reached out to embrace the teen, a touch of disbelief in her response as she pondered her reaction. "Of course I will, honey, as soon as I can, I promise."

Stephanie could only pray that Roni would hold true to her word because she wasn't crying for herself, but for her uncle. She had seen the hurt in Dean's eyes when Roni said she was going home; and even as he crossed over to stare out of the window, she knew that no one else would ever know how he felt about the situation and it broke her heart.

CHAPTER 11

▼

As predicted, Roni was barely released from the hospital before she returned to work, disregarding Dean's many objections, those she'd been turning a deaf ear to since she'd announced she was taking a shower and going to the office. Stopping outside Mason's door, she gave him a hard look and finally interrupted his protestations with a saccharine sweet smile. "If you haven't figured it out yet, we're here, so you can stop bitching about me coming in."

Dean snapped his mouth shut when Mason opened the door to usher them in, waiting for it to close before he embraced Roni, his greeting exuberant. "By God, it's good to see you up and about. When did you get out of the hospital?"

Plopping in a chair, Dean's voice was full of sarcasm when he answered for her. "About two hours and fifteen minutes ago."

Roni could only glare at him, as Mason's reprimand was so swift. "Jesus, Roni, get the hell out of here and go get some rest. This case is closed, you know."

Unable to resist the childish act, Roni stuck her tongue out at Dean before turning towards Mason as he sat down behind his desk. "Other than the constant henpecking, I'm fine. I want to go to the crime scene, Mason. I still need answers and I'm ready to finish what I came here to do."

Mason's quick glance had stopped Dean from interjecting, his tone apologetic when he responded. "Sorry, kiddo, not this time. Forensics worked through the night and has already finished processing the scene …"

Though she tried, Roni was unable to hide the disappointment in her voice when she interjected. "All of it?"

Mason's gaze was unwavering as he answered her with carefully chosen words. "Given the circumstances, yes. Things had to be handled swiftly and quietly. We have the evidence we need to close our case. Everything else is out of my hands."

And on it's way to Britain, no doubt. Opening her mouth to confirm her suspicions, she grinned when Mason continued, his tone implying that he'd anticipated her question. "We issued a press release an hour ago stating that our suspect, Nicholas Harris, was killed in a standoff after abducting another victim. There's no one outside the team that knows of Wade's involvement, and we plan to keep it that way. Understood?"

Clearing her throat nervously, Roni took a steadying breath before giving him a shaky smile and a nod. "Well, can I at least help with preparing the files for storage—anything to give me a feeling of closure here?"

Mason could relate to her request. A lot of agents didn't feel a sense of completion until the paperwork was finished; and knowing her perfectionist nature, he couldn't deny her. "Yes, Donavan, that you can do. I also need you both to write a case report for the files. Lyn's in the control room and I'm sure she'd appreciate the help."

$$*\qquad*\qquad*\qquad*$$

Lyn was indeed glad to see them, her greeting warm and sincere as she rose to hug Roni. "You look tons better. How are you feeling?"

Giving her a nod, Roni grinned, her finger's light on her collar. "Amazing what a ton of makeup and a good turtleneck will do for ya." Eyeing the plain, black boxes scattered on the table, she didn't wait for Lyn to comment before she continued. "Black-boxed, huh? Classified?"

Stretching her back, Lyn rolled her eyes, the work of the last 28 hours finally catching up with her. "Yes, which means every piece of paper has to be read before it's turned over. Procedures, you know." Giving Dean a sweet smile, she batted her eyes comically as she threw him a hint. "It would be a lot easier with some fresh coffee though."

Instead of giving her flack for reducing him to coffee fetcher, he actually surprised her with his offhand praise as he left the room. "Hell, after all the paperwork you've done, I'll bring you the whole pot."

As soon as Dean cleared the room, Lyn grabbed Roni's arm, her tone hushed as she pulled her over to the end of the conference table. "Look, Mason wanted me to seal this up before you got here, but I think you need to see it." Opening one of the black boxes, she pulled out an envelope and handed it to her, continuing with her explanation as Roni opened it. "When Wade killed Harris he not only took everything, he also took pictures of the original crime scene. Whether he planned to keep them, show them to you, or what, he ended up using them as a blueprint to duplicate Harris' flat. We found all of these amongst the pictures plastered on the walls at the house. Some were new, most were old, but one, one was different from all the others ..."

Roni's hand stilled and the blood rushed from her face as she interjected, holding up the suspected photo for Lyn's confirmation. "One male?" When she nodded Roni continued, looking at the post mortem picture of her sister's killer as she sat in the nearest chair. "Wade said he killed Harris for ruining his life." For some reason, envisioning Wade taking that photo made the weight of his actions, and her involvement in them, a bit overwhelming, and she fought for composure. "But Harris didn't do that, I did. Everything he knew about this case he had crammed down his throat by me—his patterns, procedures ..."

Lyn leaned in from the chair she'd taken, her hand covering Roni's as she fidgeted with the envelope and struggled with self-control. "While it's safe to say Wade grew to share your obsession with this case, you should not share his guilt. Somewhere the lines of reality blurred for him and he became every government's worst nightmare, an assassin with a personal vendetta." Taking the file from Roni's hand, Lyn stood to return it to its box, her soft words heavy with meaning. "For you, your biggest challenge will be putting this behind you and getting on with your life."

Roni scarcely nodded in agreement, her reply barely audible. "Yeah, I'd say so."

*   *   *   *

By late afternoon on the second day Roni and Dean were finishing up when Mason entered the control center, his smile full of kindness. "Is that the last?"

Roni thumped the top of the box, her nod slight. "Yup, that's it. You're finally rid of me."

Mason smiled broadly, his eyes reflecting the opposite of his response. "Thank goodness. I almost had an international incident on my hands, thanks to you. When's your flight out?"

Roni swallowed the lump that rose, clearing her throat nervously. "Tomorrow morning."

Mason nodded, his sharp eye not missing the reaction Dean had to the news. Stepping forward to shake her hand, his voice was not in jest this time but sincere. "We appreciate all you contributed. You were a compliment to our team, and if there is ever anything you need, don't hesitate to give me a call."

Roni returned his handshake with a firm grip, glad her voice was still hoarse, because it was a good disguise for the emotion clogging her throat. "Thank you, sir, and the same to you."

Mason gave her a nod, pointing to Dean as he turned to leave. "My office, 9:00 AM tomorrow. We need to prep for your hearing."

Dean nodded, the shock of Roni leaving making words impossible. He wasn't prepared for her to be leaving so soon and the news had hit him harder than he'd expected. Roni waited until Mason was safely out of earshot before turning to confront the pout staring at her. "Don't look at me that way."

Shrugging slightly, Dean didn't bother to hide his disappointment. "I thought you'd stay a couple more days at least."

Roni gave him an apologetic smile, her tone full of sincerity. "I'm sorry, my itinerary was delivered by courier a couple of hours ago and actually, with all that's happened, I'm surprised it wasn't accompanied by armed escorts." Her attempt at making a joke failed and she sighed heavily as she walked around the table. Stepping over his outstretched legs, she sat in his lap, chuckling at the shocked look he gave her. "Oh, what? It's not like everyone in this building doesn't know what's going on between us. It distinctly sounded like your boss dismissed you for the rest of the day, and you know what? We can do anything, and go anywhere we want."

Dean fought the grin that threatened. He could just hear her next words, and voiced them before she had the chance to. "So we shouldn't waste the afternoon sitting around pouting about tomorrow."

She gave him her most brilliant smile and a quick kiss before dragging him out of the chair. "You got it, Cowboy."

*   *   *   *

Her fork paused in mid air seconds before Roni sat it down, her low voice carrying to the sullen party across the table from her. "Come on, Dean, you've barely eaten. What is it?"

Pushing the broccoli florets around on his plate, Dean shrugged, his brow rising as he looked at her solemnly. "I just can't believe you're really getting on a plane and leaving tomorrow."

Sighing heavily, Roni took a calming breath as she picked up her wine glass. "We both knew the day would come."

Dean set his fork down and leaned forward, his voice filling with intensity. "And what about us, Roni? Are we supposed to ignore what's going on between us? Do you really think I'm going to let you get on that plane without telling you that I …"

Roni held up a hand as she fought the tears that welled in her eyes, her voice breaking with emotion. "Don't …" Taking a staggering breath she fought for the right words to express her feelings. "Don't say something you may regret later, Dean. We can't get caught up in the intensity of our relationship. We were forced into a situation that isn't natural. In a month you'll realize how boring I am and then you'd want to kill me too …"

Choking back a sudden sob, her attempt at humor failed all around as Dean's fist hit the table with a jarring thud. "Stop it! Don't try to analyze my feelings and don't compare me to that bastard. I know what I sense, and it's not the adrenaline, Roni. It's everything else, everything that we have in common: the hours we spend actually talking and laughing, it's how you make me think, and God knows even as much as I've fought it, the way you make me feel."

Roni stared at the wine swirling darkly in her glass as she fought the lump in her throat, the hurtful honesty in her response causing the tears to spill over her lashes. "I know it took a lot for you to be open with me about your feelings, but I'm sorry, I just don't know what I feel right now, Dean. I can't…." Deal with it, and even as the thought went unspoken she excused herself and practically fled the table, the confusion warring in her head and heart finally too overwhelming for her.

Leaning back in his chair, Dean sighed in frustration and was thankful he'd had the foresight to make their last meal at home. He had anticipated her reaction but knew in his gut he'd regret it for the rest of his life if he let her leave without telling her how he felt. He knew he was pushing it, knew that she was too fragile right now to handle the extra weight; but he still had to tell her, make her understand.

Roni was still fighting her demons when Dean joined her on the balcony, the sweater he draped around her shoulders serving as only a fraction of the warmth he provided as he pulled her back against his chest and cradled her within his embrace. For long moments they stood together looking out over the twinkling lights of the city, a light falling snow lending to the tranquility of the scene before Dean broke the silence with a soft whisper. "I know you're hurting, Roni. I know you're angry and confused and you don't know who to trust anymore, but I also want you to know that I'm here. When you're ready, I'm here, no matter how long it takes."

Turning in his arms, Roni looked up at him with the intent to speak but choked on the knot of emotion clogging her throat. Expressing herself the only way she could think of, she pulled him into a soulful kiss, hopeful that he would understand her gratitude. Little did she know, the open honesty in her gaze had told him more than that, because yes, although he did see fear and uncertainty, Dean also saw the love she felt, and it was for him.

✳   ✳   ✳   ✳

Roni glanced at the bedside clock, her chin quivering as she leaned down to kiss Dean's cheek. She just hadn't been able to tell him her flight was so early. She didn't think she could do the whole goodbye thing; she just didn't have it in her right now. Wiping the tear that fell on his cheek, she bit her lip as he wallowed deeper into the pillows, his face relaxed in sleep, so handsome, so peaceful. With a shaking hand she propped up the letter she'd been writing for the last half hour and quietly left the room, her feet sluggish as they carried her out of the apartment.

When she stepped from the building, the trunk on the waiting limousine popped open and a uniformed driver came around to take her suitcase and garment bag. "Your flight is expected to leave on time, Dr. Donavan. Your anticipated arrival in London is about four o'clock and Patrick will pick you up at the gate."

Roni adjusted her purse as she threw her briefcase in, her thank you automatic and without feeling. Her father had thought of just about everything.

Two hours into her flight Roni picked up her briefcase to look for something to read, her eyes filling with tears when she opened it and saw the gift left for her inside. Sometime after she had finished packing, Dean had slipped one more thing into her luggage, and her hand shook as she pulled out the portable CD player. Sliding on the headphones, she sighed heavily as the music instantly engulfed her, wondering if he had any idea how much she appreciated his gift. Who was she kidding? Of course he knew, because even after such a short time together, Dean Colby could read her like a book.

About to close the case, she caught the glint of silver and stopped to pull out a picture frame, her brow furrowing at the post-it note attached. It read, 'I liked this one.' Pulling the note off, she bit back the sob that rose in her throat and held the picture to her chest as she silently cried. One of the less obtrusive pictures taken was at the gym, and Dean had developed the shot of them sitting toe to toe on the old wooden bench in front of the ring. The smiles were natural and warm, their fingers encircled around the water bottle they passed between them. She remembered the moment and the words that made her smile like that. If the picture hadn't been in black and white, she was sure her face would have been flushed with color.

Fighting the panic that rose in her throat, she unfastened her seatbelt and rushed to the lavatory, positive that the first-class portion of the airplane did not care to be disturbed by her breakdown. Turning on the faucets, she sank to the toilet and let herself cry, thinking it ironic that at a time when she should be the happiest, she was heartbroken. She knew the day Dean had stopped her from walking out of the range that she would be in trouble, but she had walked head-long into that den of lions anyway. Now she was feeling the pangs of leaving her heart in apartment 5D of an old brownstone in downtown Denver.

*   *   *   *

When her flight landed in London Roni was back in control of her emotions, her cool composure a convincing façade for outsiders. She just hoped it was enough for family. Walking the ramp to the gate, she took one last steadying breath before facing reality, her eyes almost instantly finding her brother's, as his head was sticking up almost a foot above everyone else's.

Seconds later she was engulfed in a bear hug that was just a little harder, and a lot longer, Patrick's smile finally breaking the emotional moment. "Welcome home, little sister. Did you bring me anything?"

She socked him in the shoulder, her expression playfully hard. "I brought you the light of your life, you ingrate."

Patrick sobered completely, the rough sound of her voice reminding him of her ordeal. She had looked so normal walking toward him, but the closer she got, the more he could see the traces of blue under her makeup, and he reached out to pull at the high neck of her sweater.

Roni scowled as she slapped his hand away, her voice angry. "Don't make a big deal."

It enraged Patrick to see the ugly purple collar she wore, his grip on her unconsciously tightening even though he kept his tone light. "Look's like hell, kiddo. It reminds me of the time I got clotheslined riding my bike down Pike Street ally. Do you remember that? Old Mrs. Ryan running down the ally screaming, "Lilly, he's killed himself for sure this time!""

Roni laughed, nodding as memories of the incident flooded her mind. Her brother could never resist a dare and had paid the price for it that fine summer day. She wished her scars would heal as quickly, but she was afraid she'd wear her mark long after the bruises faded.

Patrick gave her a nudge as the shadow crossed back over her eyes, his voice intentionally bright. "Hey, everyone's waiting at the house. You can't believe how proud the folks are. Da's cooking and Granny's even here."

Roni's eyes brightened as her voice turned hopeful. "Granny Finn is here? How did you ever get her out of Ireland?"

Patrick turned from the baggage carousel, giving her a strange look. "Roni, don't downplay what you did. Don't you understand how important it was to Granny and every other old fart over there, that it was you who tracked Emily's murderer down? They don't give a rat's arse about teamwork. It's still an eye for an eye to them, and you've avenged the family name."

Roni sat on the nearest bench, starting to run a hand over her face and stopping herself. Her cover job on the bruises was questionable enough by this time. "I didn't do anything, Pat. Wade killed Emily's murderer."

Patrick gave her a shrug, his tone telling her it was useless to contradict the story. "Not what I heard." Taking a breath, his voice lowered as he looked away. His feelings about that subject were still pretty raw, so his sincerity was forced. "Sorry 'bout that, by the way, but he never deserved you."

Roni's reply was sympathetic at best. She couldn't defend Wade, but it wasn't entirely his fault either. "He didn't deserve to be turned into a monster though."

The look in Patrick's eyes was even harder than his tone when he glanced at her. "He got what he deserved. You know he told me once that he thought being married to you he'd have the perfect marriage, like our parents. I knew right then that you were doomed and I told him so, because he didn't marry Mum, he married Da." He chuckled when she hissed a Gaelic slur at him, his tone turning teasing. "Oh whatever, you know you're just like him."

Resisting a groan, she sighed heavily and gave him a withering look, steering the conversation away from the unpleasant subject. "So you're telling me that at a time when I want nothing more than to go home, take a hot bath, and sleep for a few days, I have to go to the house and put on a happy face?"

Patrick grabbed the suitcase she pointed to, his expression sympathetic. "Yeah, that and Da's study is full of suits. I figure they're planning a debriefing party for you. Sorry 'bout that too, kiddo."

Grabbing the garment bag he pushed at her, she sighed heavily as she rose. She had more than expected it; she just wasn't sure when or where they'd show up. "It's okay. I guess it's better to go ahead and get it over with. Afterwards, I'm sure

Da will have a good chew, and then, maybe, I can have a shot of whiskey and a nap."

Patrick walked her through customs, the ID's they flashed making the event as easy as walking through a door. "See, that's where you separate the pros from the rookies. You have the shot before Da gets to chewing your arse, and then another afterwards to nurse the ego. Wanna go by Murph's on the way? I'll buy you a shot and a pint and you can bend your brother's ear for a while until you find your smile again."

Roni was nowhere near ready to talk about anything so she forced a small grin and shrugged it off to fatigue. "Maybe another time. It's just jet lag. I'll be fine after a good night's sleep."

Patrick rolled his eyes and shrugged. The puffiness of her eyes wasn't from jet lag, and neither was the pain he saw there, but if she wasn't ready to talk, he knew better than to push. "Yeah, sure, another time. Besides, I'd get my arse kicked for kidnapping the guest of honor and I'm starving."

His comment triggered thoughts of Dean, and Roni nodded in agreement, averting her gaze as pain stabbed through her heart. She was going to have to get a grip on herself if she was going to make it through the night. It wouldn't do for her to be falling apart every twenty minutes in front of her family. She was relieved when her brother retreated to casual conversation about his and Shaun's latest pub escapades, enough to keep her entertained on the drive to her parent's house.

*   *   *   *

Shaun was jerking her out of the truck before she could open the door, her squeal lost in his gregarious laughter as he engulfed her in his embrace and swung her around like a rag doll. Struggling for a breath, she was relieved when her mother showed up to rescue her, even if she was overly dramatic about it.

Lillian's voice was scolding as she steadily whacked her son with a dishtowel. "Shaun Allen, put her down. Good God, she's just gotten out of the hospital!"

He and Roni rolled their eyes at the same time, his grin instantaneous before kissing her noisily on the cheek and sitting her down. "I'm glad you're home, brat. Now maybe Da will get off my arse for a while."

Roni shook her head as she chuckled, her retort full of jest as she welcomed her mother's embrace. "Yeah, like that's ever happening."

Kissing her mother on the cheek, she hugged her tightly, her reprimand gentle. "Don't make a fuss, Mum. I've been out of the hospital for days and I'm fine."

Lilly pushed her daughter back, her hands gentle on her cheeks as she studied the damage done to her gentle features, shedding tears of joy for being able to hold her daughter again. Roni saw the emotion in her eyes and gathered her close again, her soft voice reassuring when Lilly started crying. "It's okay, it's over and I'm home now."

It took her father to get Lilly to let go of her, his gruff command teasing as he nudged his wife. "Jesus, woman, let her go so her old man can have a turn."

Roni saw the glint of tears in her father's eyes as he pulled her close and wasn't surprised when she heard his gruff apology in her ear. "I'm sorry, sweetheart, for everything."

Giving him an extra squeeze, she kissed his cheek, her low reply full of sincerity. "It's okay, Da, I understand."

With a quick glance at the plain, black sedan in the drive she sighed heavily, her fingers intertwining with his as she started for the house. "Let's go get them out of here."

$$*\qquad*\qquad*\qquad*$$

It took over two hours for Roni to answer the plethora of questions that awaited her. She hadn't been prepared for the combination of her superiors and Wade's, and in the end she found herself even more exhausted, and surprisingly, on extended leave from work. She still wasn't quite sure if that had been her decision or theirs, but either way she was a little relieved. Although there was part of her that wanted nothing more than to bury her emotions under work, she knew she couldn't depend on her concentration and she was afraid she would hinder more than help.

Leaving her father to tend to their departure, Roni found her way to the small den off the kitchen, the cheery little fire in the grate welcoming her as she entered the room. Walking to her grandmother's chair, she knelt in front of her, leaning forward to embrace the ninety-plus-year-old woman, her soft voice clogged with tears. "I've missed you."

Wise old eyes searched hers as Granny Finn took her face in her old gnarled up hands, her voice full of emotion as she kissed her cheeks and responded. "And I you. We are so blessed to see you home."

Roni opened her mouth to say something and choked on a sob, hot tears streaking her cheeks as Finella pulled her into a tight embrace and assured her she would be okay. It was the reassurance that Roni was waiting on because she knew if Granny said it, it would be true. Maybe it wouldn't be tomorrow or next week, but for the first time she had hope that eventually she would be okay.

*   *   *   *

Setting her brush on the antique, cherrywood dressing table Roni ran her fingers over the finish as she looked around the room. She had caved rather easily to her parents' insistence she stay over. She liked the security of her old bedroom, of being in her family home; she just didn't know if she could sleep in it, her nerves were on edge and she was restless. Her gaze settled on her mother as she moved about making the bed, her excessive chatter going unprocessed in Roni's mind as she interrupted. "I'm sorry."

Pillow tucked under her chin and case in hand Lillian stopped and looked at her daughter strangely, her response slightly muffled. "What?"

Sighing heavily, Roni rose to walk over to the bed, her voice dropping as she sat on the wide footboard and looked up at her mother. "I said I'm sorry, for everything, Mum; for not listening to you when you told me not to marry Wade, or when you told me not to get involved with Em's case, for lying to you, worrying you …"

Lillian picked up the scattered contents of Roni's briefcase, her arm encircling her shoulders as she sat beside her, her voice calm and understanding as Roni fought for composure. "You stop that right now, Veronica. I'm sorry you had this experience, but you don't owe me or anyone else an apology. This was not your fault. No one would have ever anticipated that Wade would harm you, or anyone for that manner. You need to let this go, put it in the past where it belongs."

Covering her face with her hands, Roni's sigh was full of frustration. "I quite possibly drove my ex-husband to murder. How can I let it go?"

Lillian had automatically started straightening the things in her lap and had stopped short when she pulled the thin, silver picture frame to the top. Her mother's curiosity was instantly piqued at the picture before her. "You can start by telling me about this?"

Roni nearly groaned to open her eyes and see her mother holding the picture of her and Dean, her attempt at impartiality failing miserably as she nearly lunged for the photo. "Dean's just a friend …"

Dodging her daughter's grabbing hands, Lillian grinned as she studied the picture, her retort full of teasing. "Ummm, yes, a very good friend, I bet."

Nearly choking on the emotions that clogged her throat, Roni dropped her gaze, her defensive reaction just what Lillian had hoped for. "I don't want to talk about Dean right now."

Sighing heavily, Lillian set her things aside, her tone just as stubborn. "And I don't want to talk about Wade either. That's the past and we're not living in the past anymore, isn't that what you've been preaching to me? It's not okay for you to wallow in self pity if it's not okay for me."

There was something heartbreaking in the look Roni gave her right before she burst into tears, and Lillian knew at that instant her daughter's dilemma. Wrapping her arms around her, she let her cry, her comments more or less rhetorical. "You love him. Veronica, at least have enough courage to admit to yourself how you feel. Why did you even come back?"

It was a small muffled answer but Lillian still heard it. "I had to come home."

Pushing her backward Lillian took a strong grasp of her arms and forced some spirit into her words. "No, sweetheart, home is where your heart is, and yours is still with him. Don't stay here because of me or your father. Our only wish for you has been happiness, no matter the sacrifice we have to make." Reaching up to wipe the tears from her cheeks, Lillian forced some lightness back into her voice, her next remark making Roni laugh. "Live where you want, dear, just make sure you have a room for my very long visits."

After her mother left Roni found their conversation plaguing her mind, too many questions making sleep impossible. Could a fresh start in a new country cure her woes? Could she live without her family? Would she be a coward if she broke her own stipulations and called him? After all, she was the one that had asked for a month with no contact. With a frustrated groan she glanced at the clock on the nightstand and made a decision, leaving her room and walking down the hall to her Granny's, hoping she was still awake. Tapping lightly on the door, she whispered into the semi darkness, "Granny, are you awake?"

Looking toward the bed, she frowned not to find her there, smiling with relief to locate her sitting in a chair in front of the fireplace, a book in her lap, and a glass of whiskey on the side table. She swore by a shot a night. "There you are."

Finella nodded to the matching chair and Roni then noticed the glass sitting beside the empty chair. "I've been waiting for you."

Roni gave her a sidelong look as she crossed over and sat in the chair, pulling her legs underneath her before picking up her glass. "Sorry I was late then. Did you want to talk to me?"

Shaking her head, her wise eyes saw so much more in her granddaughter than the last time she'd seen her. She had changed, and she'd grown. "No, I think you wanted to talk to me."

Roni's eyes filled with tears and she took a sip of the amber liquid, shivering as the liquor burned a path to her stomach. The good thing about Irish whiskey was if you made it past the first drink you had it whooped, and Roni emptied her glass on the second.

Staring into the flames of the fire, she played with her glass, her eyes blurring as the tears gathered and she spoke. "Wade killed those girls to make me come after him, to open my eyes to my life and how obsessed I was with my family and my career." Taking a shuddering breath, she looked at Granny to see that her expression hadn't changed. She just sat there patiently waiting for Roni to continue, so she did. "He got what he wanted, Granny. I've been so consumed by this that now I don't know what to do. I expected to feel a sense of accomplishment, of closure, instead I feel so empty and alone."

Finella motioned her over and Roni happily obliged to sit on a cushion at her grandmother's feet and lay her head in her lap. It was something Granny Finn had always done when they were hurting.

Touching the fading marks on her granddaughter's pretty face, Finella kept her eyes diverted from the ones on her neck. It pained her too much to look at them, the thought of her going through that experience too much for her to bear. "First you need to take it easy on yourself. You haven't had time to adjust to the time change, much less the ending to a chapter of your life. This has taken a lot from you but you have come out the better person for it, you just may not realize it yet. And as for what to do now, well, for now, I think you should get away from here, away from the city and your father's silly business. For now, we should go home, get some flowers for Emily and spend some time on the farm. There, you can remember how sweet life is supposed to be."

The words only sparked memories of time on the ranch with Dean, but Roni's apprehension eased with the thought of the green Irish fields and she found herself suddenly grinning up at her Granny through tear-soaked lashes. "Can we leave tomorrow?"

Finella laughed, taking Roni's face in her hands and kissing her cheek loudly. "Yes, my pet, we can leave tomorrow."

CHAPTER 12

▼

Dean stepped out of the ancient building that housed Scotland Yard and looked again at the address the woman had written down on a scrap of paper. Of course, it had taken flashing his badge to three different people to acquire it, but they had finally relented and now he was off again. He was getting tired of working himself up only to be disappointed. He'd tried her home address and he didn't even get past the doorman. He was strongly informed that Doctor Donavan had not returned and he couldn't be more certain of the information. Now her office had given him a different address, her home away from home her colleague had said.

Flagging down a taxi, he threw his bag in and gave the driver the address as he got settled. With a heavy sigh he ran a hand through his damp hair, his weary eyes staring blankly out the rain-splattered window. He didn't know when, if ever, he'd felt so exhausted.

Sleep had not been his ally of late and he'd been on the go since Mason had thrown two envelopes in front of him and told him he was to leave immediately and that it was urgent. One envelope had his itinerary, plane tickets, and such in it; the other, marked "Personal and Confidential," was sealed and addressed to Dr. Veronica Donavan, C/O Scotland Yard.

After he had recovered from his initial shock he had tried to ask Mason about the nature of his assignment only to be met with the typical Mason brush off, "It was on a need to know basis," which meant he would find out when Mason was ready. With the look he got, he didn't push the matter. If he had a chance to see Roni again so soon, he was going to take it because the waiting was killing him.

The scenery before him began to change. The lawns expanded and the houses grew as the city faded away. Dean rubbed the dull throbbing in his temple as the car slowed and turned into a gated drive, his heart rate increasing the closer they came to the stately manor. Realizing they had given him her parents' address, he wasn't sure he was ready to face them after almost letting their daughter get killed.

The cabbie cleared his throat and Dean looked at him with a blank stare, shaking the cobwebs out as he gave the driver what he hoped was enough money. Grabbing his bag, he climbed out of the car, his heart hammering at the thought of seeing Roni again; but then, after two failed attempts he decided it best not to get his hopes up. With a calming breath he rang the bell, looking back over his shoulder as the cab pulled away. It was a pleasant entrance, nicely landscaped, a mixture of vehicles littering the drive. Turning back, he was surprised to see a woman standing there calmly studying him, although he hadn't heard the door open.

He smiled at her and could have sworn he saw a look of recognition cross her face. "Sorry, I'm looking for Veronica. I'm Special Agent ..."

She reached out and grabbed his arm, her wide smile, so much like Roni's, startling him. "You're Dean, I know who you are. Come in out of the drizzle. I'm so glad to finally meet you. How was your trip?"

Dean stepped into the foyer and sat his bag down, his hands automatically smoothing his wrinkled clothes. "It was very long. I apologize for intruding on you, but I have some documents for Roni. They told me at the Yard she would be here. I ..."

He stopped when she raised a hand. "She's not here, she's at the farm. I'll be glad to take you there tomorrow morning, if that's okay with you."

Dean shook his head, his protestations falling on deaf ears. "Mrs. Rourke, I didn't come here to put you out. I'm sure I will be able to find it if you just give me the address."

Lillian laughed, the thought of him finding the farm the best joke she'd heard all week. "My name is Lillian, or Lilly, and unfortunately, Roni is in Ireland at my mother-in-law's. My husband is out of town until tomorrow evening or he could take you; however, I was going tomorrow anyway if you'd care to tag along." Watching him process the information slowly, she smiled, the weariness of his eyes a testimony to his long trip. "You'll need to get some rest though. It's quite a trip and you look like hell. You are more than welcome to stay in Roni's room."

Dean could only smile and nod in agreement. For some reason he just knew this was what Roni would be like at that age and he loved the thought of it. "I can see where Roni gets her charm. If you're sure it wouldn't be too much trouble, I'd love to hitch a ride, and you are right, I am dead on my feet."

With a smile and a nod Lilly dragged him off to the kitchen to feed him and, of course, to pick his brain. Her casual way of making conversation and knowing what questions to ask to make him more comfortable were an art to her and it wasn't long before he was telling her everything she wanted to know. In the end she had what she needed, she knew he was a good man and that he was head over heels for her daughter.

Then again, getting a good look at Dean in the flesh, she'd totally understood the mood her daughter had sulked off to Ireland in and hoped she too had come to her senses. The cup of hot tea she gave him after his sandwich was half gone when the yawns grew longer and more frequent and Lilly gave him a small smile, her mothering tone cutting through his near senseless babbling. "I think I should show you to your room now. You can take a nice shower before going to sleep."

Dean tried to shake the haziness from his mind, following her up the back stairway to the second floor. He couldn't understand after being so wired just an hour ago how all he wanted to do now was to go to sleep, but he sincerely hoped he could make it through a shower before he did.

✳   ✳   ✳   ✳

Halfway through the Cessna flight to Wicklow, Ireland, Dean was glad he had gotten a good night's sleep because he wouldn't have survived Lillian's flying the previous day. When they bounced to a stop on the little airstrip, he resisted the urge to kiss the asphalt when he deplaned. Upon finding his knees wobbly he did however opt to lean against the wing to catch his breath.

Lillian found him there and with a tsking noise shook her head. "Oh, it wasn't that bad. I think you all just put on. So I guess you won't want to ride with me anymore either? Go get your bag. The car is in the hangar."

As she walked past, Dean shook his head as he squinted against the morning light. "Lilly?"

Turning, she gave him an expectant look, her expression full of sass. "Hmmmm?"

"Please tell me you drive better than you fly."

Rolling her eyes, she muttered something akin to "smart-ass Americans" before walking away. Dean chuckled as he grabbed their bags and followed her to the hangar, glad that he had been able to meet Lillian under such personal circumstances. The short amount of time they'd spent together had made him more at ease and they spent the drive to the farm talking and laughing, her sense of humor already very familiar to him.

Stepping from the old truck, Dean stared slack-jawed at the ancient stone and wood cabin styled house in front of him. Flowering vines climbed the stone banisters of the wide front porch, the big fat cat snoozing on the old wooden swing adding to the homey charm.

He had turned to look around the yard when his ear picked up the talk from the foyer and he turned towards Lillian's aggravated voice. "What do you mean she's not here?"

He was not getting back in that plane.

Granny Finn shook her head in exasperation, her heavily accented words hard to follow. "The first two days she spent in the flower beds, pulling weeds and pruning the rose bushes, and still she walked the floors at night. Now she just goes out with Dell and works until she drops. I don't know what's wrong with her, she won't talk to me anymore."

Turning to close the door, she finally noticed Dean in the doorway, her brow rising as she pointed at him. "Who is that?"

Shaking her head, Lillian grabbed Dean's sleeve and pulled him forward, her tone absent. "Where are my manners? Dean Colby, this is Finella Rourke. Granny, Dean is a friend of Roni's."

Dean resisted the urge to step back from the intensity of her blue eyes as she leaned forward to get a better look at him. "Friend? Bah, I see Veronica is not the only stubborn one here. Set your bags in the parlor, go through the kitchen and out the back door. I'm sure you can find your way to the barn from there."

At his confused expression she smiled slightly, giving him a nudge as she offered a bit of an explanation. "She'll be in shortly to make sure I eat lunch."

Thinking it par for her nature Dean grinned and followed Granny's instructions, chuckling to himself to hear the question she posed to Lillian as he left. "What in the world is wrong with young people these days?"

Passing through the large, old-fashioned kitchen to the back door, his momentum slowed as he stepped onto the large, stoned deck, his eyes wide with amazement at the view. The garden walk started at the foot of the porch, the neat cobblestone path weaving a pattern through the flowers and shrubs to the large gate at the rear, the bright climbing flowers on the overhead trellis reminding him of the paintings Lyn had in her office. Closing the gate behind him, he followed the same path until the barn came into view. Standing nearly as large as the house and made from the same stone and hardwood materials, it was an impressive structure.

The white fences surrounding the barn housed some of the most beautiful horses he'd ever seen, their worth evident in the structure of their magnificent heads. His interest piqued, he continued to the barn and stopped as he listened for the sound of human occupancy. Finding none, he strolled around to get a better look and he had to give it to them, their collection was beautiful, a little pricey for his taste, but not everyone preferred a good quarter horse.

The breezeway ended at open pasture and he stood, his shoulder hitched against the frame and looked out at the vast green fields. There were little dots of color clustered here and there, and he wondered if they were cattle or all horses. He decided he would make Roni take him riding tomorrow to find out, after all, it was her turn to take him exploring. Turning, he abruptly stopped as a trio of kittens scurried across the foyer. One, obviously the toughest, stopped, arched its little back, and gave him a good hiss. He laughed despite himself, surprised that the kitten didn't run as he approached it. The other two, peeking from under a stall door, looked petrified; this one looked intrigued. Scooping up the ball of fur, he found a nice spot on a couple of hay bales and acquainted himself with his new friend, hoping Roni wouldn't be too long.

*　　　*　　　*　　　*

Dell frowned up at his help, his old face wrinkling way beyond her memory. "Dammit, lass, pull it tighter. Don't let it spring up and bite ya."

She shook her head, the wire biting her hands through the gloves. She didn't know what was wrong with her. "I know, old man, don't you be biting my head off. I've almost got it."

Seconds after she completed her sentence, the tension broke and sprang back to slice her arm and Dell was quick to show his temper. "You need to take yourself back up to the house and sit with Finn if you're gonna act like an old lady. I told ya not to ..."

Roni cut him off with a look and an angry hiss, walking over to his old clapboard truck to tend to her wound. He appeared moments later, silently taking her bandanna from her and wetting it down with water. She flinched when he applied the cloth but didn't utter a sound, her eyes focused on assessing the damage. "You okay, lass? You have been extra preoccupied today."

Roni squinted up at him and shook her head, her voice strained. "I don't know, I just can't seem to get focused. This is a scratch. Some of Granny's salve and it will be good as new."

Dell finished cleaning the long scratch and after dousing the rag again, tied it securely around her upper arm. "Go home, get some rest. After all, that's what you're supposed to be doing anyway."

Roni took a deep breath and exhaled slowly, scooting off the end of the truck. "Maybe you're right. I haven't been sleeping very well lately."

Letting out a loud whistle, she picked up the bridle lying on the bed next to her saddle. Dell shook his head as the fat buckskin trotted out from the tree line, making his way to his owner. She had raised him from a foal and was the only one who could even get a saddle on the monster, he was so spoiled. "You ask me, that's the worst display of horseflesh on the island."

Roni leveled him with a glare as she slipped the bridle easily onto her horse, giving Crash a scratch under the chin. "Nobody asked you, old man."

*   *   *   *

Back at the farm Roni reigned in her horse, sliding off his back as he came to a halt at the rear of the barn. Her feet had barely hit the ground before Crash was pushing her with his head, begging for her to remove the bridle. With a laugh she unfastened the bridle and slid it off, scratching his ears as he continued to bury his head in her stomach and rub furiously. He had picked up the habit as a colt and had never grown out of it. The only problem now was that he had tripled in size.

Roni yelped as the voice came from behind her, her heart slamming into her stomach before she had time to turn around. "I never thought I'd be jealous of a horse." Dean smiled at the total and complete shock on her face, hoping she wouldn't be mad that he hadn't given her the full month she had asked for. "But at least it's a good horse."

Roni blinked again, still unsure if she was really awake or if she was dreaming that Dean was standing in her barn holding the kitten that had shredded every other person except her in the past three weeks. He held the said kitten up with a grin, his voice betraying a hint of amusement at her obvious bewilderment. "Cat got your tongue?"

Roni shook her head slowly, her voice a bare whisper as she fought the lump in her throat. "I'm scared."

Dean put the half-sleeping kitten down and gave her a slow smile as he closed the distance between them. "Now what in the world could you be scared of?"

He'd stopped an arm's length away and she knew he was waiting for her to do the rest. She'd asked for a month to get her thoughts together but it had only taken a week to know she loved him terribly and missed him twice as much. She gave him a slow smile, her eyes sparkling with unshed tears. "Of waking up ..."

His mind at ease and his heart hammering a little harder, he reached out and pulled her into his arms, his hand cradling her cheek as he looked into her eyes. "Baby, if this was a dream, you wouldn't be wearing clothes and I wouldn't have gotten into a plane with your mother. But your lips would still taste like heaven."

Roni barely had a chance to take a breath before Dean took it away, his lips devouring hers with a hunger that only she could satisfy. Roni didn't know which had triggered the tears, the sheer pleasure of the touch of his lips, his sweet words, or the notion that he'd braved a flight with her mother, but it was several moments before either one of them noticed the tears streaking her cheeks.

Dean's brow furrowed as he wiped the wetness away with a thumb and she shook her head and gave him a teasing smile. "I'm just so happy you survived that flight with my Mum."

He chuckled at her doubtful tone and lowered his head to kiss her again, crying out when their heads were unceremoniously clunked together as Crash soundly rammed his forehead into Roni's back. Giving Dean a sympathetic smile, she rubbed her forehead as she nodded toward the horse nibbling on her shirttail. "Sorry 'bout that."

Dean nodded absently and gave the quarter horse a good pat as he looked inquiringly at Roni's arm. "You okay?"

Roni couldn't help the broad grin that lit her eyes, the happiness in her voice making him chuckle. "Yes, I'm perfect. This is just a scratch."

Dean nodded and took Roni's offered hand as she started walking her horse to his stall, noting that from the second her fingers threaded with his, he felt a sense of relief, a sense of normalcy that had been missing in his life since she'd left. Taking a breath to calm his nerves, he pulled her a little closer, reveling in her admission as she squeezed his waist. "I've missed you."

Not sure he'd find his voice cooperating, Dean nodded in agreement as she walked past and he slid the half door to Crash's stall closed. Leaning his arms against the top, he watched Roni break down her gear, knowing if he offered help he'd get "the look" for doing so.

Unfastening the saddle's cinch, she easily hoisted it onto the door beside Dean, her voice quiet and sincere as she looked him in the eye. "I really have, you know? I'm sorry for leaving the way I did. I just couldn't think there ..."

Diverting his eyes, he looked at the hand she laid on his arm, his tone a little guarded. "And have you been able to think here?"

Stepping a little closer, her grip tightened and brought his eyes back to hers before she answered softly. "Yes, I have, but it seems only about how much I love you."

It took him several seconds to get his heart out of his throat, but still his retort sounded a little choked. "Well damn, it's about time you fell to the Colby curse."

Even though he made light of it, Roni could see the happiness in his eyes and responded in kind. "Well, sorry it took so long, but I do appreciate you showing up so I could admit it."

Dean handed her the brush on the hook outside the door as she laughed, his demeanor changing as he thought about his assignment. "Actually, I was sent. I'm told I'm here on official business."

She raised a brow and the brush stopped in mid stroke. "But you don't believe that?"

Dean reached into his pocket and pulled out the brown sealed envelope he'd carried halfway around the world and admitted what he'd suspected all along. "No, I don't believe it. I think Mason sent me here under false pretenses just to get rid of my—what'd he call it?—my mopey ass. I'd be willing to bet you this envelope is empty and he was just forcing a confrontation between us."

Roni gave him a speculative glance and wondered how it was that she hadn't seen him in over three weeks but felt like she had seen him at breakfast. "He didn't tell you what your assignment was?"

Dean grinned at her and gave her his best Mason impersonation. "Take this to Donavan and we'll discuss the rest when you get back."

Roni nodded as she finished up her grooming and handed him the brush as she picked up her saddle. Dean could only wonder what was going through her head as he followed her into the impeccable tack room, not surprised to find a spacious office set off to the side of the well-organized area.

Roni set her saddle on an empty wooden horse and walked into the office, looking at him with a crooked grin as she leaned against the desk and extended her hand for the envelope. "So you're willing to bet, huh? What are the stakes?"

Dean's eyes sparkled with mischief as he placed the envelope in her hand, his grin full of charm, his heart overloaded with hope. "Hmmmm, lets say if it's empty, then Mason is right and I'm useless without you, so you have to come back to the States and marry me. If it's not empty, then I stay here, suck it up, and marry you …"

Roni's brow rose as her breath caught in her throat, all joking aside when she looked at him speculatively. "What if I don't want to stay here? What if I want to live in Denver?"

Sighing dramatically, Dean rolled his eyes at her, a grin tickling the corners of his mouth. "Whatever, wherever …"

Nodding slightly, she looked at him thoughtfully, her tone turning more serious. "Empty, I marry you. If not, you marry me? Those are mighty high stakes. Are you sure you want to lay all that on the line?"

Dean took a steadying breath and passed on the offered out, his grin spreading as he winked at her. "Never make a bet if you can't pay the debt. I'm good for my part."

Roni fanned the envelope as she chewed on her lip, a grin pressing at the dimples in her cheeks. "You sound pretty sure of the outcome of this bet."

Dean shrugged slightly, amazed that he could be so glib when his heart was hammering like it was. "I know a slam dunk when I see it."

Roni took a breath and extended her hand to seal the bet, her eyes sparkling with amusement. This had to be one of the strangest proposals in history. "You're on, because I don't believe he'd send you around the world empty-handed."

Dean's brow rose as he motioned toward the envelope, his retort full of mockery. "Well, there's only one way to find out."

Roni gave him a playful glare as she broke the seal on the envelope, her brow furrowing to see the single business card at the bottom. Pulling it out, she read the message Mason had scrawled on the back that read, 'You broke him, you fix him. Let me know where to put your desk.'"

Looking up at Dean's expectant gaze with a grin, her voice was full of humor as she handed it to him. "You're a big fat loser, baby."

Her glib response sent his heart soaring and with Mason forgotten, Roni found herself actually swept off her feet, his passionate kiss smothering her squeal of surprise and squelching any doubts she had about giving her heart so freely.

Returning to earth moments later, Dean pulled away just enough to look at her fully, his brilliant smile ruining what was left of her already wrecked pulse before he brought tears to her eyes with his words. "No, I'm the winner and I will be every day that I get to hold you in my arms and show you how much I love you."

Roni pulled him forward to kiss him softly, her whispered words bringing a smile to his lips seconds before he strove to fulfill her request. "Can you start now, Cowboy?"

978-0-595-44499-1
0-595-44499-7

Printed in the United States
89828LV00005B/38/A